PEERLESS FLATS

BY THE SAME AUTHOR

Hideous Kinky

ESTHER FREUD

PEERLESS FLATS

HARCOURT BRACE & COMPANY
NEW YORK   SAN DIEGO   LONDON

For David

Lisa, her mother and her brother Max were dogsitting for a woman called Bunny, who owned a house in the Archway. Bunny was away in America and was due back at any time.

Lisa's mother, Marguerite, went to the council when they first arrived in London. The council told her to come back when she was homeless. 'But we are homeless,' Marguerite had said. 'We're just not actually on the streets.' She explained about the dog who was an Alsatian and needed three meals a day.

The council said to come back when she was absolutely homeless. When there was no roof of any kind over her head.

Lisa walked round to see her sister Ruby. Ruby was living two streets away with a boy called Jimmy Bright who dressed like a rockabilly in a white T-shirt and brothel creepers and wore his hair greased into a quiff. Ruby said that most people were terrified of Jimmy Bright. Jimmy despised the human race, with the exception of Ruby. 'He won't mind you either,' she reassured Lisa, 'cos you're me lil' sis.' Ruby's accent had flourished in the two years since she left home and moved to London.

As Lisa walked up to Jimmy's flat, she could see Ruby

sitting on the floor in a sea of crumpled clothes. It was a ground-floor flat that opened on to the street with a wall-sized sliding window. It was part of an entire row. Orange brick maisonettes with square, open gardens, and more were being built on the streets on either side. Jimmy didn't have curtains in his flat, and as Lisa approached through the derelict patch of garden, Ruby looked up and caught her eye.

'Hi, babe.' She didn't stir as Lisa slid the door.

'Where's Jimmy?' Lisa half expected him to rise up out of the debris and stop her in her tracks with his razor-sharp tongue.

'Dunno.'

Ruby was wearing a shirt with seven dwarfs all fucking each other on the front. Lisa sat and stared at it and wondered when it would get handed down to her. Everything Ruby had eventually got handed on to Lisa. Ruby was very generous with her things, while Lisa was a hoarder by nature and found it hard to part with almost anything. She had once kept a box of plain chocolates she had won at a raffle, and didn't like, on the top shelf of her cupboard for two years. Eventually they had been discovered and distributed to the family as an after-dinner treat. Lisa pretended to be angry but really she had been relieved.

'How's Mum?' Ruby asked.

'All right.'

Marguerite and Ruby rarely saw each other and when they did, more often than not they argued. Lisa acted as their go-between. It was since Ruby left home, Lisa thought. Or before: since their mother's marriage to Swan Henderson . . . since Max was born . . . since . . . Lisa wasn't sure. She could remember Ruby and her

2

mother getting on, somewhere in the distant past, but hard as she tried she couldn't place the memory.

Lisa had visited Ruby regularly in London while she waited for her sixteenth birthday. 'Don't tell Mum about this,' Ruby always ordered when they parted, and her mother's first question was inevitably, 'So how is Ruby getting along in London?'

Ruby was so unspecific as to what exactly she was to keep quiet about that Lisa never knew how to answer. 'Fine,' she said, and then at night she would lie awake, worrying that if something terrible happened to her sister, it would be her fault for withholding vital information. Now that Lisa was in London herself she understood why Ruby had come back to school for the Christmas Fair, only six months after leaving, talking and swearing like a native East Ender and wearing a T-shirt for a dress and heels so high she couldn't walk down the hill to the pub. There had been no shortage of lifts on offer. Cars Lisa had never seen before swung open their doors.

Ruby was meant to be in London on a History of Art course. By the end of the first term she had already dropped out and was working in a shop that sold bond-age trousers and plastic shorts and shirts with one sleeve longer than the other. People were whispering that Ruby was on drugs. That she was having an affair with a Sex Pistol. That it was a sacrilege to cut off that beautiful waist-length hair. Lisa felt immeasurably proud.

Ruby stood up and began searching the floor. 'Bastard,' she said, 'he's taken me fags.'

Lisa had a packet of ten John Player Special in her pocket. She smoked John Player because they had a 'scratch and reveal' lottery in every packet to which she

3

was addicted. She offered Ruby one. Ruby slouched through to the kitchen and smouldered it against the electric ring of the cooker until it caught.

'Mum wondered if you wanted to come round and have supper with us tonight,' Lisa said casually, passing on a message, investing nothing of herself in the request.

'Yeah, I might.' Ruby pulled on her cigarette and changed the subject. 'Jim's old man gets out of the nick next week.'

'Oh.'

'This, you see, is his gaff.'

'Does that mean you'll have to move?'

Ruby sank back down to the floor, her thin, white legs crossing. 'Jimmy says we can all live here, he says his dad's all right. But I'm getting out.'

'You could come and stay at Bunny's,' Lisa said into the silence because she couldn't bear not to, and when Ruby didn't answer she added, 'but then again . . .'

'Yeah.' Ruby let her off the hook. 'Anyway, you'll be moving on yourselves soon, won't you?'

'That's true,' and Lisa stretched out a hand for a drag of Ruby's cigarette.

On the day Bunny returned from America, Lisa's mother went back to the council. Lisa took Max to the park. Max was five and was only really interested in foxes. Foxes were his main subject of conversation.

'Look, there's a red fox in the pond with a fox tail and no ears and it's hungry and I'm going to eat you for my dinner. Are you a fox? I like foxes. I might be a fox when I grow up.'

Lisa tried to focus her mind on what he was saying and even attempted to answer his less obscure questions.

'How long is a fox tail?'

'Hmm, I don't know.'

'Is that fox very bad? Bad fox. Bad fox.'

'Quite bad.'

'Are you a fox?'

Lisa's patience never lasted long. 'No I'm not a fox. PLEASE be quiet.'

'But if a bad fox came out of a hole in the ground in the middle of the night . . .' Max talked very fast with his words close together and his eyes staring straight ahead. It made Lisa feel crazy.

'Shut up.' She shook his narrow shoulders so that his teeth chattered. He continued anyway: 'there's a red f-f-fox and a bl-l-lack f-f-fox and two very big foxes-s-s . . .'

Lisa gave him a final shove so that he fell back on to the grass with a thud. 'Shut up-p-p.'

'Shut up-p-p.' Max mimicked her exact tone and she

5

knew that she was only winning because she was stronger than him. From the day Max learnt to talk he always won with the last word.

Lisa slumped back into the grass. 'I'm sorry.'

Max stared straight ahead with his flat black eyes.

'Would you like to know how to make a deluxe daisy chain?' she asked him.

He rolled over and waited while she reached around her, collecting the longest-stemmed daisies. He had a pale pointed face with two bright red patches on his cheeks like a child's drawing. His hair fell straight and black over his forehead in exactly the same way as his father's had. Lisa thought how strange it must be for her mother to be reminded daily of Max's father, who at this moment was setting off on a round-the-world sailing trip with a Dutch nursery-school teacher called Trudi.

When they arrived home, Marguerite was waiting impatiently for them. 'They've given us a flat. They tried to put us into bed and breakfast, but then at the last minute they came up with a flat, a temporary flat, until they house us.'

'Bed and breakfast . . .' Lisa murmured mournfully. 'That could have been lovely.' Lisa had always longed to spend the night in a hotel, but to live in one, like a Parisian intellectual . . .

'You don't understand,' Marguerite said, 'it wouldn't be like that.'

Peerless Flats was in Peerless Street and was, as it turned out, just behind the Old Street roundabout. It was a faded 1930s block with stone staircases and bay windows and was hemmed in on every side by tower blocks. The man from the council was waiting. He glanced dubiously at the expectant faces of Marguerite and Lisa as they trailed after him with their plastic carrier bags of clothes.

There were two olive-green doors on either side of each landing. Max ran from door to door head-butting the wood and shouting, 'I am the Foxman, I am the Foxman,' but no one appeared to complain.

The man stopped on the fourth floor and unlocked a door, and for a moment they all stood crowded together in the tiny hall of the flat. The council man showed them wordlessly around. He pushed a door open into the sitting-room. It was oblong and empty, with wooden floorboards and a window with small panes that cut the tower block opposite into squares. There was a bathroom and a narrow kitchen with flowers in orange, brown and yellow on the wallpaper all linked together with hairy green stalks. Max covered his eyes when he saw them. At the end of the kitchen was a toilet in a little room that hung out over the edge of the building.

The man from the council stood in the middle of the kitchen and clicked his tongue between his teeth.

'Where are the bedrooms?' Marguerite asked.

7

The man widened his eyes as if he hadn't quite caught the gist of the conversation.

'There seem to be some rooms missing,' she said.

The man checked his form. 'You have been allocated a temporary homeless one-bedroom flat.'

'Well, where is it?' Marguerite demanded to know. 'This one bedroom, where is it?' And she kicked open the bathroom door to prove her point.

Lisa gulped. She hated a scene. 'Mum, it's fine.' She felt her ears tensing up and her head filled with a high whine like a dying light-bulb.

The man walked briskly into the sitting-room. 'In council terms this is a one-bedroom flat,' he said, and then noticing Max, swinging viciously from the handle of the toilet door, he softened his tone, 'but I must ask you to remember, this is temporary accommodation and you will be rehoused in the shortest possible space of time.'

He handed Marguerite the keys and left.

They returned the next night in the van loaded up with furniture. Marguerite had driven to the country to collect the things they had left stored in a garage until they had a place of their own. There was an iron bunk bed and the wooden base of a bed that had long since lost its legs. A fridge, a gas cooker and a tall wooden cupboard Marguerite had had for nearly twenty years. They had packed their books into boxes and the rest of the clothes from Bunny's into plastic bags.

As Lisa and Marguerite struggled up the staircase with the bed base between them, Lisa caught sight of some-

8

thing on the first landing, something oddly familiar. Marguerite stopped, jutting the frame into Lisa's side. 'Darling, aren't they yours?' she said, and in a horrible instant Lisa recognized a pair of her knickers. A green and white striped pair, the ones with the elastic gone in the waist. She nearly let the bed slide away from her down the stairs.

'I don't know.' She pushed to go on. 'Mum. Please.'

'But how did they get there?' Marguerite insisted.

At the same moment they both remembered the bags of clothes they had left propped against the wall of their new sitting-room. Marguerite stooped down and hoisted up a smudgy vest of Max's. 'Mum,' Lisa begged, and they began to heave on up.

In silence Lisa passed various grimy items that had once belonged to her. The sleeve of a jumper she had been knitting infrequently since she was twelve. It lay ragged in the crook of the stairs, collecting dust and cigarette ash, and still attached to its ball of wool by a long thread that wound its way down the staircase and out on to the street. Lisa disowned it. She cracked a little pot of blusher with her foot as she continued up.

The door of their flat was unexpectedly shut and locked. Lisa held Max back as they hovered in the doorway and listened. There was not a sound and so they ventured in. Apart from the missing clothes, there was no other sign of a break-in.

'There's a fox swimming in the toilet,' Max shouted from the other end of the kitchen, and when Lisa went to investigate she found that the toilet door was locked. It was locked from the inside. If there is a fox in there, Lisa found herself thinking, he's gone and locked himself in. She felt the skin on her face tighten as the door refused

9

to give. She had a creeping feeling that there was someone holding on to the handle from the other side. Her
hand trembled as she unclasped it and backed away.

'Mum.' She wanted to stay calm for Max's sake. Max
latched on to a person's fear and his black eyes spun and
his voice was louder than was bearable when he
screamed.

'Mum . . .' Lisa called, 'I think there might be someone
in the toilet.'

Marguerite strode over to prove her wrong. She took
hold of the handle and pressed down and pushed up and
banged on the door with her fists and called with her
face close to the wood. 'Hello. Is someone in there?
Hello!' The more she shouted the braver her voice
became. It even created a hollowness that echoed back
at them through the wood. 'It must just be locked from
the inside and someone very small must have climbed
out of the window.'

'Someone tiny,' Lisa agreed, thinking of the window,
which she remembered as being one square pane of glass.
The size of a rabbit hutch. 'Someone rabbit-sized,' she
suggested, and stopped herself as rabbits and thieving
foxes, borrowed from Max's bubbling brain, began to
chase across her mind.

They knocked, as a family, on the door of their neigh-
bour. A young woman answered, pulling her matted
wool dressing-gown across her chest as she inspected them
through a slice of door.

'We've just moved in at number 52,' Marguerite told
her through the crack.

The woman swung open her door. 'Well, hello.' She had a high, Irish voice. 'I'm Frances.' She was as pale as milk with a turned-up nose and skinny, skinny hair. 'Well, there's a hell of a crowd of you.'

Lisa nodded. 'But it won't be for long. They're going to rehouse us as soon as they can.'

The woman smiled encouragingly. 'That's true all right. There's few that is here longer than three years.'

'Three years,' Lisa gasped. 'We were thinking more of three weeks. The man said —'

'Oh the man!' she interrupted. 'Your man said I'd be out of here before the baby came and Brendan was to come over for the birth, but little Brendan is all of six weeks now and I've not heard a word.'

With that, little Brendan, as if hearing himself called, set up a thin wail from the other side of the wall and Frances hurried away to comfort him.

Frances's flat was identical to theirs, with the same layout and overpowering wallpaper. The gas fire in the sitting-room was blasting and the oven door was open, steaming up the hall and kitchen with a heat that made the empty flat feel full. Frances invited them to take a peep at little Brendan, who lay quietly staring at the ceiling with his blue-rinsed eyes that were waiting patiently to change.

Lisa held Max at arm's length. Max hated babies and was liable to shout into their faces. Max only had respect for children older than himself. Unless they had turned into old ladies. Old ladies he took special pains to kick as he passed them in the street.

'Isn't he lovely?' Marguerite cooed, and Frances beamed with pride.

'It's just a great shame his father's not here to see him.' Frances flopped down on to the bed. 'But if he comes over before they offer me a flat, we'll never get a place of our own. It's our only chance.'

'Couldn't he just come over for a visit?' Lisa asked, but Frances stared miserably into the fire and didn't answer. They sat for a moment in silence until the crash of a chair falling in the kitchen roused them. Max had been trying to get at a half-eaten Milky Way on the draining-board.

Frances offered them the use of her toilet. 'Just knock three times,' and she laughed conspiratorially.

She stood on the landing with Brendan in her arms and kept guard while Lisa and Marguerite unloaded the rest of the furniture. They squeezed one half of the bunk bed into the bathroom as a bed for Max, in case he could be induced to go to bed before them, and set up the other half and the wooden base in the sitting-room. Lisa spread the beds with blankets that were as familiar to her as anything she knew. They had made more homes than she could count feel like home with their unfolding. Frances brought them through cups of pale tea and they stood around chatting and smiling, and all the while straining for sounds of the burglar breaking out of the locked room.

Lisa and Marguerite lay against opposite walls pretending to be asleep and keeping their fear to themselves. The wooden window-frame creaked with every shock of wind and sent waves of possibilities through Lisa's chilled body. She listened so hard she thought her bones might crack. She twisted carefully in her sheets and heard her mother do the same.

Lisa tried to remember when she and her mother had last slept in the same room. Not since she was a child and had slipped out of her own bed, wading through the silk of a black dream to climb in with her mother. Not since her mother had moved upstairs, first herself, then her few possessions, to Swan Henderson's shrine-like room with the king-sized mattress and the roll-top desk where, years later, Ruby had found the love letters addressed to 'Trudi, my sweet'.

Lisa, Ruby and Marguerite had moved in with Swan Henderson as lodgers. They had moved in during the summer holiday when Lisa was nine. For almost a year they had been living in a large house on a bend in the road between one village and the next. It was a bend where cars frequently crashed. It was famous for it.

'We've been living here for ages,' Lisa had said to her mother as spring approached and she watched for the first time as her own daffodil bulbs, planted in the autumn, burst into flower. 'We've been living here for ages and ages. I'm bored,' Lisa tried again to prise a reaction from her mother. Lisa put a moan into her voice, although she wasn't sure how seriously she wanted it to be taken.

'I want to live in a house with my own garden so I can plant a blue rose bush and watch it grow up,' she had complained when they packed up from their last place and moved for the eleventh time in three years; but a part of her liked the excitement and the new people and a different bedroom and a different garden and a different lift to school almost every month.

'It looks like we will be moving,' Lisa's mother said, interrupting her thoughts and taking her by surprise. 'At the end of the summer term.'

'Where to?'

Marguerite didn't know. 'But as always,' she said, 'something is bound to turn up.'

Lisa woke up with a start. The sun was streaming through the uncurtained window and her mother was still asleep with her face to the wall. Lisa's whole body ached and the moment she moved she was reminded of the locked room and the chair they had left jammed against the toilet door.

Max sat cross-legged on the kitchen floor absorbed in a game of Lego. Lisa tiptoed over him. She shifted the chair and tried the handle. Nothing had changed, but in the light of morning the locked door looked less sinister and she tapped at the wood happily with her fingers as she made her way to the bathroom to take a pee in the sink.

Lisa dressed Max and then herself and, taking her brother with her for safety in numbers, she walked out into Peerless Street to find a shop to buy some bread and milk for breakfast. It was Sunday and a strange, empty calm hung over the boarded cafés and the pillared basements of the tower blocks. Peerless Flats itself was still asleep. She kept a hand on Max's shoulder as they wound down the staircase, avoiding the litter of her most personal belongings, and even kicking her green and white striped pants into a narrow corner as they passed. They wandered hazily into Bath Street and through to Ironmonger Row, where they discovered a Turkish baths and a laundry but no shop. They walked slowly back across to City Road and turned in towards the Old Street roundabout. Max was unusually quiet, and stayed by Lisa's side, keeping up with quick padding steps of his plimsolled feet.

'I wonder if anyone except us lives round here,' Lisa said, and Max looked up at her with blank eyes.

There was a row of bus stops at the end of City Road with buses that went to the Angel and Highbury Corner. There was one bus, passing every twenty minutes, according to the timetable, that went up to the Archway and stopped at the end of Bunny's road. Lisa was tempted to wait for it and travel in its warm, red comfort to an area where people lived and shops opened, but she thought of her mother waking up in the empty flat alone with the locked room, and she hurried on around the roundabout, scanning side streets for signs of life and peering into the deserted squares.

Marguerite stirred as she slammed the door. 'Did you get some milk?'

'No.'

'The foxes are dead,' Max explained, and for once Lisa was inclined to agree.

*

Marguerite, Lisa and Max sat at a greasy table in a restaurant at the top of City Road. It sold kebabs. Skewered, or in bread. It was the only place they could find to get a cup of tea.

Max was very excited and drummed his hands on the table. 'Oh let him have a 7-Up,' Lisa pleaded and Marguerite wearily raised her hand to the waiter and ordered.

Max drained his drink in one furious slurp. He then set about chasing each remaining bubble and destroying it with a shriek and the butt of his straw.

'First thing tomorrow morning,' Marguerite said, 'I'll go down to the office and tell them we have to have a bigger flat. And I'll get them to do something about that door.'

Lisa nodded. She was thinking how she'd be starting college the next day, and her blood rippled hot and cold at the thought.

'And if they won't rehouse us,' Marguerite let her voice trail off, 'we'll just have to think of something else.' Lisa listened absent-mindedly. She was wondering how she'd prepare for her first day without the use of a mirror. 'Something is bound to turn up,' she said and she smiled her mother's own reassuring smile.

Lisa was meeting her father for supper. She was glad to have an excuse for going out and she took the tube into the West End. Lisa rarely saw her father without Ruby. Secretly she thought of him as Ruby's father and felt uncomfortable about seeing him alone, even a little treacherous. After all, it was really only Ruby's tenuous link that bound them together.

They were having dinner in a fish restaurant. Lisa arrived to find her father sitting drinking Pernod with a girl she knew. 'Hello, Dad. Hello, Sarah.' She stood awkwardly at the end of the table.

'Oh, has it been raining?' her father asked, and Lisa looked down at her bedraggled coat and the boats of her shoes and wished she had washed her hair.

The waiter pulled out a chair and tucked Lisa in with a thick white napkin opposite her father. Sarah crinkled up the eye nearest her in a smile. Lisa ordered a Pernod too and picked at the radishes and bread sticks that adorned the table.

'I was just walking along and I saw your father leap out of a taxi,' Sarah laughed, and then added, 'I hope you don't mind, I'm starving.'

Lisa didn't mind. In fact it was nice to have a buffer between her and her father and the inevitable pauses.

Sarah was a year older than Lisa and she had known her on and off since she was seven. They had met at an Easter-egg hunt in Wales in the garden of Sarah's family home, where Lisa had had the great luck to meet up with the owner of a telescope – a man who led her to various eggs nestling in the low branches of trees, on window-ledges and scattered in the grasses of the outer lawn. Lisa had collected so many eggs she couldn't hold them in her arms and a bag had to be found to carry them.

'Are you living in London now?' Lisa asked Sarah, and Sarah said she was working in a clothes shop on the Fulham Road. She stood up to show Lisa a pair of maroon corduroy jodhpurs she had bought there at a discount.

'And how about you?' Sarah asked. 'How long have you been in London?'

'Three weeks.' Lisa felt anxious about having a conversation that didn't include her father. She looked at him from time to time and smiled expansively. 'I'm doing a drama course. At a college in King's Cross. I'm about to start any moment.'

The waiter arrived to take their orders. Lisa's father ordered oysters and so did Sarah, but Lisa couldn't quite bring herself to the challenge and asked for a prawn cocktail. She knew it was a childish and unsophisticated starter but she loved the sweet pink mayonnaise of the dressing, and in a defiant mood she followed it with fish cakes.

Lisa sat at the table and blushed to think how she had suggested only the year before they meet for supper at the Wimpy, Notting Hill Gate. She had seen its red and glass exterior from the top deck of a bus on several visits to London and her longing to go there was overpowering. Brought up in the country on a diet of brown rice and grated carrot, a cheeseburger and chips were her idea of gourmet delight. The Wimpy had in fact turned out to be a success and Lisa even heard her father exclaim over the deliciousness of the hot apple pie spiced with cinnamon, served in little cardboard packets.

Sarah and Lisa's father were discussing the people on the next table. Sarah giggled and pointed out the sharp line of the man's curling, auburn wig. The woman, Lisa's father said, looked as if she had been recently discovered under a large rock. He said it was enough to put him off his oyster. Lisa sweated for them.

'Ruby sends her love,' she attempted to pull the conversation around.

'Oh, how is Ruby? I haven't been able to get hold of her.'

Lisa explained about the flat, and Jimmy Bright's father getting out of jail, but it turned out that Ruby hadn't mentioned Jimmy to their father and he was under the impression she was living with a girlfriend.

'Oh, well maybe she is . . .' Lisa didn't want to betray Ruby's confidence, let alone disagree with her father. 'Well, she probably is by now.'

Lisa drained her Pernod.

'What's Ruby up to, anyway?' Sarah asked.

'Music.' Lisa jumped at the question. 'She's going to be a singer. She's got a friend who says when he can find a band talented enough to play with her . . .' Lisa broke off. She was only repeating what she'd been told. It was strange how much more convincing things sounded in other people's mouths.

'I think I bought her a guitar last Christmas,' her father was saying, and Lisa nodded, knowing he had, and knowing also that it had been stolen or swopped or lent to someone glamorous like Mick Jagger's brother or a roadie from The Clash.

Lisa's father insisted she try an oyster. 'Just swallow it, with a passing bite,' he said.

Lisa swallowed it so fast that she didn't even get a chance to graze it with her teeth and she was left with the sensation of having sea water in her mouth and a pebble on her heart.

'Not quite sure about that,' she said with a grim smile.

Sarah slurped her oysters joyously. 'It's an acquired taste.'

Lisa braced herself for news of Sarah's brother Tom. Lisa had been in love with Tom, among others, ever since she could remember. Once, on a holiday in Wales, they had lain together on a tartan blanket, Tom, Sarah and herself, and she and Tom had held hands and talked about how many children they would have when they were married and what they would call them. She couldn't remember the names they had chosen now, but there were to be three and they had been in complete agreement over every last detail of their upbringing. Lisa could almost see the stars in the black sky, how they had looked that night. Clear and calm and full of promise.

'You know when you stick your finger up your bum?' Tom had asked.

'Yes . . .' Sarah spoke as if she were waiting, and eager, for him to continue.

'Lisa?'

'What?' She unclasped her hand.

'What I just said.'

Lisa refused to be drawn. She stood up and wandered off across the lawn to lean against a box hedge as high as the first floor of the house. She hated conversations like that. She couldn't help herself.

'So how's your brother?' Lisa asked eventually when the waiter had cleared away the plates. 'How's Tom?'

'He's fine.' Sarah looked at her with a sly expression that made her wish she'd kept the question to herself. 'He's learning about farm management in East Anglia. He's living in a cottage on the estate with Lenny. In domestic bliss.'

'Who's Lenny?' Lisa's father asked for her.

'Lenny is a man Tom met at the Marquee. He's black and incredibly good-looking and Tom thought it would be fun to have someone around to keep him company.'

'So what does Lenny do all day when Tom's at work?'

'It's hard to tell,' Sarah laughed. 'The last time I went down there I arrived at four in the afternoon and they were both still asleep. I can't help feeling that Tom probably isn't cut out to be a farmer.

It was only once they were out in the street that Lisa realized how drunk she was. Her head felt as though it was full of cotton wool, and her ears wouldn't pop.

'Which way are you heading?' her father asked her, hailing a taxi.

'Old Street,' she said.

The cab stopped and Lisa's father kissed her very lightly on the forehead. 'Do you mind if I take this? I'm meant to be somewhere.' And he glanced at his watch. He pressed a twenty-pound note into Lisa's hand. 'Will you take the next one?'

Lisa nodded.

'Goodbye. Goodbye, Sarah,' he said and he jumped in.

'Thank you . . . and thank you for supper,' Lisa shouted through the closing door of the cab and she waved at his back in the low back window as he sped away.

Lisa and Sarah walked towards Leicester Square. Lisa weighed up in her mind the quandary of the journey home. If she took the tube, she could avoid breaking into her twenty-pound note. A taxi might be three or four pounds, whereas the tube, especially if she got a half ticket, would only cost her ten pence. Lisa was small anyway and if she bent her knees and looked with wide eyes into the little window – 'half to Old Street please' – she found it never failed.

'If I were to buy some trousers like yours, how much would they be?' she asked Sarah.

'About nineteen pounds.'

'You wouldn't mind, would you? I'd get a different colour.'

'Listen,' Sarah said when they reached the station. 'I'm going to stay with Tom at the weekend. Why don't you come?'

Lisa's heart began to pound. 'All right,' and they kissed each other on both cheeks and said goodbye, separately bracing themselves for the last tube home.

Lisa and Marguerite got up early and, leaving Max asleep in the bathroom, went downstairs to the office. The office was in the basement of Peerless Flats and the caretaker had just arrived and was unlocking the door.

'We have a problem with our flat,' Marguerite told him.

The man looked nervous. 'Which one you in, then?'

'Fifty-two. The toilet door is locked. From the inside.'

'I'll be right up,' he said, 'just give us a moment.'

'And there's something else,' Marguerite grumbled as she retreated.

'What's that, then?'

Lisa sighed and tugged at her mother's arm.

'There aren't any bloody bedrooms, are there?'

The man appeared half an hour later with a bag of tools. He inspected the door and took out a hammer with a rubber top, which he smashed against the wood until the lock snapped and gave. 'Kids,' he said. 'Frigging kids.'

The window was wide open. Lisa stuck out her head and peered down expectantly, thinking she might see a child with the face of a hardened criminal lurking below, but there was nothing in the concrete yard except rubbish thrown from the windows above by people too lazy to use a dustbin.

'Mum,' Lisa said, as she was about to leave for college, 'I'm going to go away for the weekend with Sarah.'

23

'What weekend?'

'This weekend. On Friday.'

'That's ages away.' Her mother was irritable all of a sudden. 'Why don't you tell me a little nearer the time?' As Lisa opened the door to leave for her first day at college, Marguerite relented. 'I'm sorry, it's only that – it's nothing. Good luck for today.' And she kissed her tenderly on the cheek.

'Bye, Max,' Lisa called, but he just muttered 'Frigging foxes' from the bathroom, where he was dressing himself in a suit of grey, plastic armour.

Lisa walked slowly down the long, strip-lit corridor of her college. She was early. As she walked, she rested her hand lightly on the top of her head, twisting her face into an expression of stern concentration as if she were unaware of her own actions, but all the while moving her eyes furtively from side to side to check that she was not being observed. The moment she had stepped through the main doors of the building it seemed to her that the top of her head had begun to open up. She had to keep her hand over it to stop it from catching fire or melting, and when she removed her hand it was as if her scalp were being burnt into by an ice-cube.

Lisa was always early. As hard as she tried to be late or even on time she still found herself arriving before anyone else. It was the thing that set her apart most severely from Ruby and her mother, who were both compulsively unpunctual. In Lisa's last year at school she would ring her mother from a payphone several times during the afternoon to urge her to begin the four-mile drive early enough to collect her on time. It never made much difference. Her mother would arrive in the battered blue van that had once belonged to the local butcher, swerving crazily round the makeshift school roundabout as if to dodge a crowd, long after the car park had cleared and the very last child had been collected. She arrived in such a fluster and armed with so many dramatic and implausible excuses that Lisa could never bring herself to retaliate with more than a moment or two of silence.

Lisa sat in a circle of plastic chairs in the hall where the drama classes were to be held. She rested both hands on her head as if she were purely stretching her arms. She pressed down hard on the bone of her skull to stop the clicking and the whirring in her ears and hoped to God no one would notice. She wondered whether it was the strip-lighting she was allergic to, or just the after-effects of the Pernod. She remembered hearing some-where that too much Pernod could rot your brain and send you crazy.

There were places for twenty-five students on the Full Time Speech and Drama course. Lisa had auditioned. She had been helped with her pieces by a lady her mother found called Moira Philips who lived in the next village and who at one time had been an actress. Moira Philips was blonde and squeezed tightly into her clothes. She talked in mysterious and casual tones about 'Rep' and 'Equity' and 'up' and 'down' stage. The rumour that Moira's husband had not run off with a scientology student but fallen and slipped to his death under the wheels of a barely moving train at East Grinstead station, before it was uprooted and sold to the Americans, added, in Lisa's estimation, to her status as a drama teacher, and she paid great attention to everything she said.

Moira Philips advised her to look at a book called *Audition Speeches for Girls* and she helped her choose a piece and 'blocked' it for her. Lisa hoped no one at the audition would ask her the name of the character or what play it was from, as she had taken the book back to the library before memorizing anything more than the lines.

Once everyone who was likely to arrive in the hall for drama arrived, the teacher started on voice exercises.

Lisa had never thought much about her voice before, but now it turned out she had a 'weak R' and certain vowel sounds she pronounced were wrong. Lisa couldn't hear the difference for the life of her. But the worst thing was her accent. When she spoke, the other students laughed and asked her to repeat herself as if she were a foreigner. She remembered Ruby confiding how she had practised for her college canteen, 'I'll 'ave some of them peas please . . . some of them peas . . .' and she resolved to do anything at all in order to fit in.

They stood in a circle and shouted along with the teacher. He was a small man with glasses and nylon trousers who introduced himself as Pete. He didn't fit at all with Lisa's idea of the theatre. 'Wibbly wobbly. Wibbly wobbly,' they repeated after him, stretching their mouths and their eyes and making full use of their lips.

'Bibbly babbly. Bibbly babbly. Moo ma moo ma moo.'

Once they were warmed up he led them in a round of 'Peter Piper picked a peck of pickled peppers. A peck of pickled peppers Peter Piper picked.' They ended on a string of 'Red lorry yellow lorry' and a full five minutes of 'Furious thistle', which was to be enunciated with no spit, whistle or lisp.

The drama teacher wanted the class to improvise. Bev, a short and stocky girl with dreadlocks, was desperate to go to the disco. Her boyfriend was coming round to pick her up in ten minutes. The drama teacher cast Eugene as the boyfriend. Lisa had spoken to Eugene during registration. He worked in the evenings as an usher at the theatre where *Evita* was playing, and his conversation was spiced with references to the show. At every opportunity he would break into a musical number. Lisa waited to see if he would introduce this talent into the improvisation.

Bev strode up and down the makeshift sitting-room. She cursed in full-blown patois. She was furious because at the last minute her mother had asked her to babysit. Janey was her mother. A sixteen-year-old Indian girl with a grave and world-weary expression. Bev was impressively angry. She used such strong language that even Janey was a little taken aback. By the time Eugene arrived to take Bev to the disco, Bev and Janey were rolling around on the floor in what Lisa imagined was a stage fight.

The drama teacher ended the improvisation and announced the start of morning tea break thirty minutes early.

Sarah's shop was a boutique not far from the Fulham Road cinema. Lisa had managed to keep her twenty-pound note intact by travelling half fare to college and back, and using the luncheon vouchers they handed out to each student to buy her midday meal.

Sarah's trousers were undoubtedly the highlight of the shop's collection. They came in three colours. Maroon, mustard, or a grey-green which reminded Lisa of lichen.

'You've got to have the green ones,' Sarah said. 'To bring out your eyes.'

Lisa kept them on, packing her skirt into her bag with her nightie and her copy of Stanislavsky's *My Life in Art.* They caught the train from Liverpool Street. Sarah had some grass, which she rolled into a joint under the train table. She suggested they smoke it in the Ladies so they'd be in a good mood when they arrived.

Lisa crouched up on the lid of the toilet seat and Sarah leant against the basin.

'Can I ask you a question?' Sarah said, the smoke billowing out of her mouth. Lisa's stomach tightened. Her head began to click with the first bitter inhalation of smoke. 'It's a question from Tom.'

'All right.'

'Tom wants to know . . .' And Sarah began to giggle.

'What?'

But Sarah wouldn't bring herself to tell her. 'He can ask you himself,' she said.

Instead Sarah told her about her cousin Tanya who was still a virgin and ashamed of it and was coming down next weekend in the hope that Lenny would deflower her.

Lisa hated that word 'deflower'. It made her squirm. Sarah looked hard at Lisa through the smoke and Lisa knew what she was wondering. She pulled on the joint and kept the smoke inside her lungs as long as she was able.

Lisa hadn't seen Tom for over a year and he was taller than ever and thinner. His long, grey eyes drooped at the corners. Lisa and Sarah climbed into the front seat of the Land Rover, Sarah shuffling behind so that Lisa had to climb in first and squeeze right in next to Tom. Their legs pressed against each other and the musty oilskin smell of him tingled in her nose. Sarah leant over the seat to talk to Lenny, who was lying stretched out in the back.

'How's it going, Len?' she asked him.

'Not so bad, and you?' Lenny said. Lenny was smoking, and every bit of energy in his body was concentrated in the hand that lowered and raised the cigarette to his mouth.

'Tanya sends her love,' Sarah said, and Tom sent out a peal of cruel laughter that made Sarah twist round to hide the blush that spread over her face.

They were driving out of the small town through flat, green fields dotted with barns and farmhouses and wispy autumn trees.

'So, when are you going to be a famous actress?' Tom jerked his leg against Lisa's.

'I don't know. Never, I expect,' Lisa stammered.

Secretly she hoped that she *was* going to be a famous actress, or even an actress of any kind, but after one week of Full Time Speech and Drama she couldn't imagine it.

'Don't be all floppy,' Tom broke in. 'You've got to play the part. You've got to sleep with important people and say "Darling" if you want to get anywhere. Have you got an agent?'

'No,' Lisa said.

'Do you hear that, Lenny?' Tom shouted over his shoulder, and Lenny said, 'Yes, sir.'

Tom's cottage was on a road that led past the gaunt family house of the estate. It was beyond the farm buildings and was surrounded by fields. For Lisa, an air of glamour hung over Tom's house like mist.

It was dark when they arrived. Tom opened the door and flicked on a light. The sitting-room was barely furnished but the floor was so littered with mouldering cups of coffee and dirty plates that it gave the impression of clutter. A stale smell of fried food hung in the air.

Sarah showed Lisa round the house. The kitchen was a bombsite with every piece of cutlery caked in butter or jam and each surface supporting a toppling tower of plates and pans and half-empty cans of baked beans and rice pudding. The cupboards hung open, and proudly empty.

Upstairs there were two bedrooms. An unmade bed in each. Lisa refused to catch Sarah's eye and looked instead into the bathroom, noticing a spray of blood on the wall beside the sink that made her duck back on to the stairs.

31

'It's great,' Lisa said, as she came back into the sitting-room.

Tom was making a fire with half a packet of firelighters and what looked like the remains of a chair. 'How's Ruby?' he asked.

'She's fine . . . she's . . .'

'What?' Tom watched her suspiciously and Lisa wondered whether or not to tell him how Ruby had arrived at Bunny's the night before they moved out with her arm slashed and dripping blood. She had knocked on Lisa's window and, under strict orders not to wake their mother, Lisa had walked with her to the Whittington Hospital where she received a tetanus injection and five stitches. Ruby had made her swear not to tell anyone. At the time Lisa had interpreted 'anyone' as Marguerite and their father, but that was because she didn't know anyone else in London she could tell. Tom, she felt, could only be impressed by the news.

'She got into a bit of a fight last week,' Lisa told him, lighting up a cigarette.

'With who?'

'With a bread knife.' She felt proud of that remark.

At first Ruby told her how she'd been slicing bread when the knife slipped and caught the side of her arm, but later, worn down by painkillers and the long wait in casualty, she had confessed that during an argument with Jimmy she had stabbed at herself in a moment of despair.

'Seven stitches,' Lisa told Tom, and Tom looked suitably impressed.

'You should tell her to come and stay,' he said, and his eyes softened. For a moment Lisa remembered what she had suspected since they were children, that really Tom

32

was in love with Ruby. Something heavy pulled inside her chest and she pushed the thought away. She inhaled deeply. She could feel Tom watching her out of the corner of his eye. It was Tom who had taught her how to smoke. Or at least how to inhale. Before Tom took her in hand, shortly after her thirteenth birthday, she just used to swallow the smoke, gulping it down like a drink and then waiting for a respectable length of time to elapse before letting it out again. This method of smoking invariably resulted in draining the blood from her face and making her feel sick.

'It's interesting how you inhale,' Tom had said to her. She was on holiday with Sarah and Tom's father on the Isle of Man, where all there was to do was smoke cigarettes and read aloud to each other from the *Thirteenth Pan Book of Horror*. 'You see, whereas you swallow the smoke, I breathe it in.' He hadn't said it in a sneering way and he demonstrated 'inhaling' to Lisa with all the gentleness of an elder brother. They sat by the side of the sea experimenting with smoking styles until Lisa felt so dizzy she almost fell into the waves. Tom had to hold her steady with his hand. It was the summer after that they had named their children on the tartan blanket.

Lisa waited until the last possible moment before going to bed. Sarah had gone up first with a cheerful goodnight and Lenny had followed shortly after. Eventually Tom drained his can of beer, 'I think you're staying in my room,' and with that he disappeared up the stairs.

Lisa changed into her nightie in the bathroom. She brushed her teeth and, as there was no sign of a towel,

33

shook her hands until they were dry. She noticed the blood had been wiped from the wall.

Tom was lying in bed, a long thin shape under the blankets. Lisa slipped in beside him. The moment she touched the sheets she began to shiver.

'Are you cold?' Tom asked, his voice unfriendly from the other side of the bed, and she had to stop her teeth chattering to answer.

There was nothing comfortable about Tom's embrace. When he put his arm around her, bones and the sinews of his long limbs bit into her flesh. They lay still, Lisa's neck resting in the crook of his arm, his hand icy on her shoulder. Lisa stared up at the ceiling. Her mind raced with the beginnings of a conversation. Any conversation. Tom twisted on to his side and reached his long arm swiftly down to the hem of her nightdress. Lisa doubled up and clamped her legs together and gripped his wrist with both hands. She strained with every muscle to pull his hand up above the covers. She turned on his trapped arm and faced him and dragged at his free hand with gritted teeth. Finally his resistance went and she raised his arm up like a trophy and rested it on her shoulder. Lisa's chill had left her. She could feel Tom's hot breath on her face. She folded her arms in front of her, holding them out like breakers against her breasts. Tom kept his hand where she had placed it.

Words Lisa could not get a grasp on burnt in her throat and dissolved. She leant forward and kissed Tom on the side of his mouth. She wanted him to know that she loved him whatever he did. She wanted to tell him that she didn't really care about the sex except she couldn't stand it all being over, as she assumed it would be, and then they weren't due to get the train back to

London until Sunday. Lisa released one of her hands and stroked the hair back from his face. His breath came hot and fast, and with no warning his free hand slipped off her shoulder and lunged down the front of her night-dress.

Wordlessly they fought, Lisa tugging at his iron wrists, and all the while rolling away from him with her knees bent up to jab him in the stomach. As she struggled, she caught his smile in the filtered light from the window. 'It's me,' he seemed to be saying, and she relaxed in his arms and grinned stupidly back at him.

'Couldn't we just go to sleep?' She turned and pressed herself warmly into the curve of his body.

'You should have said,' he whispered, touching her ear with his lips, and they lay awake until morning, on guard for each other in the tangle of the bed.

Lisa and Sarah walked aimlessly along the fenced edges of one field after another.

'Did you sleep well?' Sarah asked. 'Last Night?'

Lisa ignored the light in her eye and the stress of her words. 'Yes,' she said. She knew she was treading close to the edge of Sarah's patience.

They walked on in silence.

Tom had had a meeting at midday with the farm manager. He got up at five to twelve, pulled on his clothes and roared away in the Land Rover. Lenny was on a day-trip to London and wasn't due back until the evening.

'Do you think Lenny likes me?' Sarah asked when they'd walked so far in a circle that they could see the back of Tom's cottage three fields away. She sounded as if she had reason to believe he didn't.

'Of course he does,' Lisa said automatically. 'Why shouldn't he?'

Encouraged, Sarah linked her arm. 'And Tom, I know he likes you. He told me.'

Lisa decided against believing her. She couldn't imagine Tom coming that close to a declaration of love. His conversation was almost entirely made up of little cryptic phrases. 'Really?' she said.

*

Lenny arrived shortly after dark with a gram of heroin. 'H', he called it. Tom shovelled it into four lines with a razor-blade and snorted his share into his nose with a rolled-up pound note. The inside of Lisa's head began to shrink and crack and the burning ice that had lifted seeped back into her skull.

Tom smiled at her with his elder-brother eyes. 'It's all right,' he said.

Lisa didn't know you could snort heroin as if it were cocaine. Ruby, she knew, injected it into the veins in her arms. She had tried to get Lisa to share a needle with her but Lisa had lost her nerve at the last minute. Ruby was like Tom. They hated anyone to be left out.

'Come on, Lisa Lu.' Tom crawled across the floor to where she was leaning against the legs of the sofa. 'You won't regret it.'

Lisa's stomach turned bitter and she needed to go to the toilet. 'Is it like . . . like . . .' She could hardly say the word. Tom bent his head down to hers. She lowered her voice. 'It's not at all like . . .' she whispered what was on her mind, 'acid?'

'My God, not at all. It's literally the opposite,' Tom reassured her, pressing the rolled-up note into her hand.

'So you don't hallucinate or anything?' she persisted faintly.

Tom shook his head.

Lisa gave in, and sucked the powder up into her nose, using one nostril and then the other in an imitation of Tom. Tom took the magazine off her lap and patted her leg like a school teacher. He pulled a blanket from the sofa and spread it over the four of them as they lay in a circle in front of the electric fire.

'So when did you take acid?' Tom wanted to know.

37

He sounded annoyed. Tom liked the idea of having introduced Lisa to everything illegal she had ever done.

'About a year ago.'

'What was it like?' Sarah asked.

'All right . . .' and then, admitting a fragment of the
truth, she added, 'A bit scary.'

The heroin was beginning to take its effect. Lenny,
whose line had been fatter than the others, lay back with
his eyelids heavy, and a dark smile on his lips. Tom sank
his head on to his chest and was silent. As far as Lisa
could tell, it wasn't affecting her, but then the thumping
of her heart had subsided and, apart from the occasional
click, the inside of her head was as soft and safe as history.

'I had an aunt,' Sarah said, 'who took acid. Someone
put it in her drink.'

'Really?' Lisa asked. 'What happened?' A pinpoint of
fear was fighting with the milk in her veins.

'She went crazy. She tried to eat a biscuit tin and then
she walked to the nearest station and boarded a train.
She jumped off just outside Audley End.'

'Was she all right? I mean, did she ever recover?'

'Never, not as far as I know. Tom, did Aunt Bird ever
recover?'

'What?'

'From whoever spiked her drink with acid.'

Tom raised his head and looked at her with cat's eyes.
'Never,' he said, and he smiled a thin smile as if he were
in some way responsible.

When Lisa woke the next morning she was lying on the
floor, her head under the crook of Tom's arm. She scrambled free and stood up. She thought for a minute about

what she would do if the others all turned out to have died in the night, but just the very fact of having survived made her feel so cheerful that without even checking on their pulses she went upstairs to the bathroom.

Lisa locked the door and ran herself a bath. She felt thin and white, and when she lay face down in the water the bones in her hips pressed against the bath's bottom and her empty stomach lifted away like the curve of a bowl. She washed her hair and brushed her teeth and put on a clean shirt with her green trousers. She sat outside in the sun. A sense of calm spread over her body. She knew what it was. She had taken heroin and survived and now she would never have to take it again. She had proved herself. Like a Red Indian coming of age and scarring his face with warlike marks. She was sixteen and she had tried every drug she had heard of. She was free to begin her own life.

'Cup of tea?'

A shadow blocked her own private stream of sunlight. It was Sarah.

'Thank you.'

Sarah handed her a mug and slid her back down the wall. She looked over at Lisa and smiled. Lisa caught her smile just as she was raising the drink to her lips and in that instant she remembered the story of the night before. Aunt Bird and the biscuit tin. Trains and parties and drinks spiked with . . . A cold fear froze her arm midway to her lips. Her brain hissed. She set the cup down. A skin was already forming on the tea's milky top. She watched as it hardened and turned a dark rust-brown. She kept her eye fixed on it, expecting to see a tab of 'white lightning' or a 'purple haze' swim to the surface and give itself away.

Marguerite and Max were cooking pancakes. The tiny flat was filled with the smell of frying batter. Pancakes were something they had inherited from Swan. Grace before meals they had dispensed with, porridge for breakfast they had never mentioned again, but pancakes on a Sunday – that was one of the few things that remained to remind them. Max was sitting up at the table carefully stirring the batter with a wooden spoon. Marguerite was watching over the pan. Lisa stood in the doorway and watched her flip a pancake over.

'How was it?' her mother asked her.

'Fine . . .' She was glad to be home.

Marguerite told her that she'd applied for a teaching job and also that she'd introduced herself to a family of white South Africans waiting to be rehoused. They were politically opposed to the government in their country and they had given up the rolling veld and the mountains and swimming-pools of their land for a one-bedroom flat on Peerless Street. Marguerite had met them in the office during her most recent campaign for a flat with a bedroom.

'They invited us over for a drink sometime.'

'And me too, nowadays,' Max told her, stirring happily.

Marguerite smiled over his head. 'A new word,' she mouthed, 'nowadays,' and she shrugged.

'Anything for a change,' Lisa whispered and she tried to hug Max's bony and resistant shoulders.

They sat in the sitting-room with their plates on their laps and ate the pancakes, piled one on top of the other in a tower, with spoonfuls of honey and the juice of a lemon squeezed between each layer. Lisa felt as if she hadn't eaten for a week. Tom and Lenny only bought McEwan's Export and sweets when they drove into the local town. For breakfast earlier that day they had toasted marshmallows. They had pronged them with forks and held them up against the bars of the electric fire until they sizzled and melted into liquid inside a sweet brown shell. When they were finished, Tom ripped open a bag of jelly babies with such force that they had to be retrieved, one by one, from every corner of the room.

Tom and Lenny had a plan which involved Lisa. They wanted to act as her theatrical agent. Lisa thought it might be better to wait until she had finished her course and then even until after she had trained at an established drama school, especially in view of what had been said about her voice, but Tom said it was never too soon to start putting yourself about. He found a pen and made notes on a pad of paper. Age. Height. Hair. Eyes. Accents.

'Can't you do any accents?'

Lisa couldn't think of one. And then 'Some of them peas please' came into her head, and so as not to seem underqualified she said cockney.

'Be prepared for that phone call,' Tom warned her. 'It could happen any time.'

Lisa wasn't sure whether or not to tell him that she didn't actually have a phone. But then it occurred to her that neither did he. She could only assume he must have some grand and alternative plan that he would explain to her eventually.

Lisa met up with Ruby in a pub in Islington. It was a great dark room with no tables or chairs and music so loud the chords of the guitars thudded in the roof of your mouth. Lisa found her sister lounging against a wall, shoulder to shoulder with Jimmy Bright.

'Watcha, sis,' Jimmy said, and Ruby gave her a hug.

Ruby and Jimmy were both drinking Pils, and Lisa pushed her way through the crowd at the bar to buy another round. 'Same again,' Ruby shouted after her and Jimmy held up his bottle.

Lisa ordered, and watched herself in the low mirror behind the bar. The pupils of her eyes were so distorted by the dimness in the room that they had taken out the light in her eyes. She wouldn't have recognized herself, except she looked a bit like Ruby.

Lisa didn't notice until it was too late that the barman had poured the top half of each bottle into half-pint glasses. She craned to look over at the others. She wouldn't make it back to them in one go, and she knew she didn't have the courage to leave her drink unguarded at the bar. She stared mournfully at the collection of half-filled bottles and glasses. She would take the three bottles and then come back for the glasses, but as she gathered them up, the wide-open mouth of her glass changed her mind and she took two of the bottles and one glass and hoped she'd reach the bar and back again before it came to any harm on the ledge beside Ruby.

Having decided which was her drink, she hurried with it, keeping her hand outstretched over the top. She squeezed through the crowd of elbows and arms and thrust the bottles on to the ledge. 'We didn't want glasses,' Ruby grumbled, but Lisa was already slithering away through the crowd, stumbling backwards, to keep an eye, as far as possible, on the golden pool of her lager. She surfaced at the bar, turned and rushed back with her armful of drinks. It occurred to her on her way that she could have poured the beer back into the bottles and then carried all three in one go, using her thumbs and a finger as corks, but now it was too late.

'Cheers,' Jimmy said, raising his bottle, and in the confusion Lisa forgot which glass she'd marked for herself. 'Cheers,' she said, but she didn't drink.

They stood in a row, their backs to the wall, and watched the people come in off the street and squeeze themselves into the crowd at the bar. There was no room for conversation. Lisa relaxed fractionally and took a slug of lager. She regretted it immediately. It tasted bitter. Lisa couldn't help wondering if it tasted more bitter than usual. If it is spiked, she thought, I'll know in twenty minutes. Her stomach contracted. She glanced up at the clock. It was ten-fifteen. Fifteen, twenty, twenty-five, thirty, thirty-five. If by twenty to eleven her mind hadn't caved in and splintered like a sheet of glass she'd know she was going to be all right. Now that the damage was done the bottle lost its menace and she slugged at it to soothe her anxious wait.

'Another drink?' Jimmy said, heading off for the bar. It was ten-thirty. Her scalp tingled with the new dilemma. 'All right.' Her voice was so small that no one could have heard it, but Jimmy nodded and was gone.

43

Lisa thought she would faint with the exertion of waiting for the heavy hand of the clock to move. Her hands and feet were freezing and her front teeth ached.

'How's it going, sis?' Ruby shouted, inches from her ear.

'Fine,' she yelled back, her eyes stretched out with fear.

'Seen anyone, been anywhere?'

'No,' was all she could manage. 'Not really.'

She leant her head back against the wall. The inside of her skull felt like the brittle webbing of a sack. Moving and cracking and tearing with each swallow.

'Seen anything of the old man?' Ruby asked.

'What?' Lisa didn't know who she meant, and as she glanced around for inspiration she caught sight of the hands of the clock just as they were chugging noislessly into place. She had been spared. Her shoulders dropped and a sigh hissed like music through her heart.

'I won't be a minute,' she said and, taking her bottle with her, her palm pressed hard against its open top, she went to the Ladies to celebrate. She needed a change of scene and a way of escaping the gaping bottleneck of Jimmy's fresh drink.

'Hello.' A man blocked her way on the steps that led to the floor above. 'I haven't seen you here before.'

'No,' Lisa said. It sounded stupid but she couldn't think what else to say.

'What's your name?' He was from somewhere Lisa couldn't place. Up north, she thought, or America.

'Lisa.'

'I'm Quentin.' He stepped to one side. 'Sorry, were you on your way somewhere?'

Lisa said she was, but she'd changed her mind. 'It was just something to do,' she told him.

44

Quentin looked at her quizzically.

They walked back down the stairs together. 'Where are you from?' Lisa asked him.

'Belfast.'

Once they were in the comparative light of the pub, Lisa was struck almost speechless by his good looks. She was talking to a film star. He had velvet eyes and a sparkle in his face that shone even in the dim light of the pub. When he smiled, he showed his teeth and his lips formed a bow like a lion's grin.

'What do you do?' she asked him, and he winked and answered, 'Oh, a bit of this and a bit of that.' There was a tone in his voice that made her want to lean against his arm. 'You here on your own?' he asked, and with a quick glance across the bar she said yes. She would have liked to introduce him to the others, but she was scared that Jimmy would bristle into action and turn him into a fool with a flick of his tongue.

Quentin looked at her with added interest. 'You're different,' he said, and she blushed with the thrill of what she hoped was a compliment.

The bell was ringing out closing-time and the grille of the bar dragged down over the insistent heads of the last orderers.

Lisa saw Ruby looking around for her. 'Listen, I'm going to have to go,' she told Quentin, and as she moved away he caught her arm and asked, 'Will I see you again?' Lisa thought for a moment and then said quickly, 'Meet me next Friday at one o'clock outside the King's Cross branch of W. H. Smith's,' and with only enough time to register his surprise she rushed off to catch Ruby and Jimmy as they spilled out on to the street.

*

45

Lisa was glad they'd moved to London. She waited breathlessly for the week to pass. She tried to concentrate on college, and practised her voice exercises in the privacy of the toilet. 'Furious thistle, furious thistle, wibbly wobbly bibbly bobbly.' She practised rolling her R's and dropping her accent. She said 'Ta ta Max love' before setting off in the mornings.

One evening Lisa went with Marguerite to see the South Africans who were in fact from Rhodesia, or Zimbabwe as they called it when they remembered. There was a great crowd of them. There were two sisters with pale orange hair. One of them, Heidi, had a baby and it was her and her husband's flat they were all in. The other sister, who had a girl of six, had a flat in another part of the building. All the Rhodesians in London, it seemed, congregated at Heidi's and one Scottish man called Steen. Steen had the same pale orange hair as the sisters but he wasn't related.

Lisa wondered what he was doing there. His eyes were so heavy and of such a dark blue that they bulged out from under his hooded eyelids. You could see the hard-boiled egg of each eye through the thin white skin even when his eyes were lowered. Steen sat in the corner and rolled grass from a tin into a king-sized tobaccoless cigarette. It crackled as he smoked it and the acrid smell of the burning grass got inside the other smell, the sharp smell of piss and baby sick that permeated the room. Instead of covering it, it sent it swirling through the stale air. Lisa felt suddenly cold. Her feet were icy and the skin on her hands was puckered and white. Steen got up.

46

First he walked over to Heidi's husband and offered him the joint, and when he refused it, he came and sat down next to Lisa.

Lisa had promised herself that she wouldn't take any more drugs or even smoke, but here, in this silent room with her new neighbours and her mother looking on, she didn't have the courage to refuse. She took the offering and inhaled deeply, holding the smoke until the count of five so that when she breathed it out it made a thick white plume in the air. Lisa forgot about her feet and even though her head began to crackle there was a reassurance in knowing it was still there. Steen continued to sit next to her and his knees moved gently to the rhythm of the music.

'What is it?' Lisa asked him when the joint was handed back to her.

'Balham home-grown,' he said. 'Do you like it?'

Lisa nodded.

Steen fumbled deep into the pocket of his trousers and pulled out a slippery packet. It was a ball the size of a squashed tomato. It was yellow-green grass wrapped in clingfilm. He handed it to Lisa. He pressed it into her hand. Lisa closed her fingers round the warm and gristly package.

'Thanks,' she said.

Lisa wondered why it was that men always gave her drugs. The men she came across pressed dope into her hands in the same way her father pressed money. She must have a sort of orphan addict look about her. Her mother's boyfriend, after the split from Swan, had brought little packages of red and gold Leb to slip to her on his regular weekendly visits. It didn't make her like him as much as he hoped, but it did make her the most popular girl at school. It also made the separation from Ruby more bearable and she could use it as ammunition to compete against her London excesses.

Lisa didn't breathe a word to anyone about Quentin. She kept him a secret, hardly daring to say his name. She didn't mention him to the girls at college, or to Sarah when she called her from the payphone at Old Street station. She only asked if Tom had left a message about auditions for film or theatre parts. She was relieved to find that there was nothing.

'All Tom wanted to know when he rang,' Sarah passed the information on, 'was how to get hold of drugs and . . . where was Ruby?'

Lisa's money ran out and she replaced the receiver with a heavy heart. She took the short cut home. It was a narrow road that cut between two tower blocks and led into an underground car park. There was a ramp at the very end that opened on to Peerless Street. Every time Lisa took this route she promised herself she would never take it again. More than anything, she dreaded walking so close to a tower block. She felt that at any moment someone was liable to fling something from a top-floor window and flatten her as she crawled along below. The smallest thing could kill when dropped from such a height. A pellet of chewing-gum might bore a hole through the top of your head with its accumulated speed. Once, she had heard the echoey shouts of children, and on looking up she had seen two tiny, curly heads smiling miles and miles above. They were hanging at right angles over the edge of the building. 'Derr-brain

49

chicken,' they shouted, and Lisa was so sure they were going to drop a saucepan on her that she backed right up against the wall and waited for their mother to pull them in.

Lisa walked so fast that she cracked the heel of her shoe. It splintered away from the arch of her instep as if refusing to keep up with her ferocious pace. She arrived home in a sweat of frustration and burst into tears. She sobbed and gasped and bent her shoulders, and, through a stream of slimy, welcome tears, thanked God there was no one at home. Lisa ripped off her broken shoe and hurled it across the room. It sailed in an arc across the hall, through the kitchen, and landed with a thud against the toilet door. Lisa limped after it. She picked it up and in a calmer mood studied the hairline crack of the loosened heel.

It wasn't so much the ruined shoe that was the tragedy. It was the fact that she had planned to wear them for her date with Quentin. They were bright green slingback sandals with a heel so high they made her feel like someone else. She had been wearing them at the pub when Quentin had drawn her into conversation and she didn't want to shock him by turning up at King's Cross nearly three inches shorter than his memory. She had to find Ruby. Ruby, she felt sure, was the only person who could help.

Lisa left a note for her mother and took a bus to the Archway. She knew that officially Ruby wasn't meant to be living with Jimmy Bright, now that his father was out of prison, but she didn't know where else to look. She trudged through the orange-brick housing estate with her shoe in a plastic bag. It was getting dark and it amazed her how few people there were about. She had always imagined London teeming with life. She had pictured it in a continual state of carnival, never taking into account the side streets and dead ends.

Just by looking at Jimmy's flat she knew it was empty. It was dark and there was something abandoned about the great sheet of dirty glass that stretched across the window. Lisa tiptoed through the garden and tapped against the sliding door. Now she was there she hoped that Ruby wouldn't be inside. She dreaded to see her shadow rising up from the floor of that mildewed room. She tapped again. And waited. And as soon as it was safe to leave, she tiptoed back out through the garden and hurried away towards the traffic and the lights of Junction Road.

Lisa took the spiral staircase that led down into the depths of Archway station and jumped on to the first train that pulled in. When Lisa travelled by tube, she always made a special effort to ride in the smoking carriage, even if she had no desire to smoke a cigarette herself. The first time she'd come to London to stay with Ruby she had been more impressed than she could say by the chance meeting of one of Ruby's friends riding on the Bakerloo Line. They had leapt with burning cigarettes into the last carriage of the last train home, and Ruby had slumped down opposite a man in DM boots laced up to his knees. 'Oh, hi, Vic,' she had said as if it were the most normal of occurrences. She didn't even blink at the safety pin he had clipped through his nose. Since then Lisa assumed that if she were going to meet anyone she knew on a train, the smoking carriage was her only hope.

51

Lisa changed from the Northern to the Metropolitan Line and found herself heading towards Hammersmith. She was going to visit her father. She'd never called on her father unannounced before. Her fist was white and bunched around the handle of her plastic bag. 'If you see an unattended package or bag in this compartment do not panic . . .' She read and reread the compulsive warning printed opposite her on the curve of the wall. 'If you see an unattended package . . .' 'If you, if you see, if you . . .' She began to count out each letter of each word on her fingers. Unattended. She ran it off, from one hand to the next. Package. Seven letters. It took five rounds to let it finally rest at the end of her hand, to let the word trickle off her finger.

Lisa idled along a deserted street behind the closed-in stalls of Hammersmith Market. She wasn't sure exactly what it was her father did, but she knew he was a very busy man. She dreaded disturbing him in the middle of some important business. Lisa's father spent a lot of time talking on the telephone. He had a telephone with no number on it. A telephone that only rang out. He talked to people about horses and the times and towns of races all over England. Sometimes he left his telephone lying unattended on a table top and out of its black and speckled mouth would come a litany of numbers and names that meant nothing to Lisa but that filled the room with an unshakeable suspense.

When Lisa was out with her father he had a tendency to wander off, and she would find him talking through one side of his mouth to men who hovered at the bars of cafés or stood gathering information behind a stall of street-market artichokes. Lisa had once heard a woman whisper that her father was banned from every race course in Great Britain. She had said it with such awe that it made Lisa think of Ruby and the way she was revered at school. Lisa thought of this now as she walked through the dark, leafy streets. She knew the ban must be simply due to her father's invincible eye for a winning horse and the fear he could evoke in each and every book-maker.

Lisa's father lived in two rooms of a terraced house. It was a small house that was part of a square and there was a miniature playground in the middle. There were swings and a slide and a very muddy sandpit. Lisa was sure she could remember playing in that sandpit when she was a child, and sliding down the slide. Once she mentioned this to her father and he gave her a half-glance and said it was unlikely. She later discovered he hadn't moved to this street until she was ten. It must have been another sandpit she had played in. She regret-ted having brought up the sandpit or the subject of her childhood. She regretted it so much that sometimes even now she woke in the night with a pain in her stomach and a bitter shameful taste in her mouth.

The light was on in the double room that looked out on to the street. Lisa walked up the stone steps to the front door. The door was covered in graffiti. Smudged-up swear words and splashes of red paint. A board had been nailed over the letter-box and a new double lock shone out of the wooden frame. Lisa remembered that there wasn't a door bell, and now there was no longer a letter-box to clang for attention she assumed she was supposed to shout.

'Dad,' she mouthed feebly into the still air. 'Dad.'

A blind clattered open above and her father's silhou-ette appeared in the window. She could see him peering out. From twenty feet she sensed his irritation.

'Dad, it's Lisa.' It was too late to run away.

'Oh, hello.' He had both his hands on the window-sill and he was leaning out. 'Do you need something?'

He didn't want to let her in, that was all she could think of. She shouldn't have come. She should never have come. 'Oh, no not really.' Her voice rose up out of a lost part of her. She couldn't remember why she was here.

'Do you need a bit of money?'

And then she remembered. 'It's just I've broken my shoe . . .' and she realized her mistake. Of course he wouldn't know where Ruby was. She was probably out somewhere in the basement of a nightclub and if she brought up her name and her lack of address she might inadvertently be getting her into trouble. 'I suppose if I had a bit of money I could buy another pair . . .' Lisa's voice trailed off as her father slammed down his window. She waited, defeated, on the steps.

Lisa showed him the shoe. It was hard to see the crack by the hazy light of the street lamp.

'Poor you,' her father said. 'Will that be enough?'

Lisa crunched the note in the palm of her hand. 'Thank you.' They shuffled in silence for a moment and then Lisa moved off. 'Thanks so much,' she said.

As soon as she heard his door slam, she began to run. She kept the money in her hand, its cutting edge against her palm, and ran as hard as she could.

Lisa took up her position by the glass door of W. H. Smith's, the door that led out of the station and on to the street. She had to wait for some time before the giant hands of the St Pancras clock even got to one and struck, and then out of the corner of her eye she watched as the minutes jolted stiffly by. She flicked through a magazine and tried not to look. She didn't want to be surprised by Quentin while studying the time. She wanted to give the impression of a casual, calm and easy-going girl, carefree and a little scatty. She didn't want him to know she was the kind of person who counted the letters of the insides of words and arrived for appointments fifteen minutes early.

Lisa had been concentrating so hard on her breathing, and just exactly how she was going to react to Quentin when he tapped her on the shoulder, that it took her a moment or two to register the chimes of half past one. It took another ten minutes to conclude that Quentin wasn't coming. She folded her magazine and, with a gaping space where all her nerves had been, she wandered into the shop to buy herself some chocolate. It was only then that she saw the other door and the shoulder of a man leaning up against it.

'Quentin?' she ventured, and he turned around and saw her. He had an expression of impatience on his face that took a moment or two to lose. Lisa, having achieved her aim of carefree unpunctuality, let it all go in a moment of panic. 'I was waiting at the other door,' she told him, and Quentin took hold of her hand and led her out of the station.

Quentin was twenty-five and a down-on-his-luck drugs dealer. He was quite taken aback to discover Lisa was only sixteen. She felt him freeze away from her on the park bench where they were sitting. Lisa had expected this. She was used to it. She took out her trump card.

That morning she had released Steen's Balham home-grown from its plastic wrapping and it had expanded into a jungle of stalks and leaves and little seeds, enough to fill a tin tobacco box. She drew this tin out now from the pocket of her coat and without a word flipped up the lid. She slid three Rizla papers from their packet and, under Quentin's watchful eye, rolled them into a perfect joint with smooth white sides and a neat cardboard roach.

Quentin looked anxiously around the park. There was a row of secretaries eating sandwiches on a bench not far away. Lisa struck a match and, cupping the flame in both hands, she set light to the twisted ends of the paper. Tom would be proud to see her now, she thought, and so would Ruby. Quentin was impressed. Not only with Lisa's display but with the quality of the grass.

'Where did you get this stuff?' he asked her.

'Someone gave it to me.' Lisa was regaining power. 'A friend.'

'Some friends you have,' and they both leant back on the bench and let the sweep of the grass roll over them as its heady pull came and went in waves.

Quentin bought cans of lager, which they drank as they walked through the back streets of King's Cross.

'Those girls are probably even younger than you,' Quentin said, as they passed the pale prostitutes lurking on the pavements. They had bare white legs with plasters where their court shoes rubbed, and stripes of blue and pink make-up that refused to mingle with the pallor of their faces. Lisa passed them every day on her way home from college.

They were heading into Holborn. Quentin didn't try to kiss her. He just kept hold of her hand. Lisa liked him all the more for it. He had a strong, warm hand that didn't sweat or hesitate. Lisa hurried along by his side. She was wearing her green sandals, and so far, they were bearing up.

When she had arrived back from the black mistake of her search for Ruby, Max and Marguerite were at home. They had been there all the time, only next door, comforting Frances, who, Marguerite said, was losing her mind cooped up all day with little Brendan. Lisa had arrived home so numb, she could hardly turn the key in the lock.

'Where have you been?' her mother asked her. Lisa could never lie with any conviction, so she just mumbled and shrugged and sidled into the bathroom. Max was sleeping in his towelling pyjamas, and when she leant down to kiss him he was as still and sweet as a saucer of milk. Lisa had her father's folded note still clutched between her fingers. She looked at it for the first time. She sat on the end of Max's bed and stretched it flat over her knee. It had a 'one' printed on its green face. She turned it over and over, unable to believe what it was telling her. Then she remembered how dark it had been on the steps of her father's house and how, after all, it had been wrong and stupid of her to interrupt his business for something as trivial as a broken shoe. She curled up on the bed next to Max, careful not to brush against his

57

outstretched arm, and listened to the sound of her mother in the kitchen, waiting patiently for her to reappear.

Marguerite helped her mend her shoe with Sellotape and a glue Max used for sticking weapons on to soldiers. If she ran, or walked too fast, she could feel her heel bend, but now as she strode along in the grip of Quentin's steady pace she could only hear a friendly squeak.

'Would you like to see a film?' Quentin asked her. They had been walking in silence for nearly half an hour.

Lisa nodded. The way Quentin said film made her want to go down on her knees to him.

There was an 'X' called *Scum* that had just opened. Quentin said they were lucky to get tickets, but when they went inside, the cinema was almost empty. Lisa supposed it was because it was still the afternoon and most normal people were at work. The film was about a boy's borstal. Quentin said he knew one of the actors in it. It turned out to be a boy who got gang-raped and then committed suicide in his cell because the prison officer wouldn't answer his call. He cut his wrists with a shard of glass. When they found him, he was slumped against the door as if he had been calling for help until the very last moment.

The cinema was freezing. Lisa's feet were so cold she had to take off her shoes and sit with her legs folded under her. She needed to pee for the fourth time since the film began. She jigged around and tried to last out another ten minutes. 'Not again,' Quentin said as she stumbled off down the aisle.

When they walked out into the street it was dark. 'That was fantastic,' Lisa said, even though she had seen most of the film through the slats of her fingers.

Quentin put his hands in his pockets. 'I've got to see a man about . . . something.' Lisa looked at the ground and waited for him to say goodbye. She felt like a piece of sea-weed ready to be washed away. 'North London,' Quentin shuffled his feet. 'D'you want to come?'

Lisa put her arm through his and nuzzled her face against his jacket. She couldn't resist a skip as they walked. This was the beginning of something, she thought, from now on there would be life before Quentin and life after. If they were still together at one o'clock next Friday she would have a little party in her head.

Quentin led Lisa into the pub. It was the pub that she had met him in. She bought him a pint of Guinness and herself a Bloody Mary, because even though she didn't want to stop drinking, she thought she'd better have something more filling than lager. Quentin took his Guinness and wandered off to find his man.

Lisa stood at the bar and looked at herself in the mirror. Tonight she wasn't frightened of anything. She sipped at her drink and abandoned herself to love.

There was a band playing live in a room below the pub and Quentin took her down to listen to the music. Wherever they went, he kept hold of her hand for everyone to see. The man on the door, who was a large, very black man with a shaved head, had some kind of business with Quentin. They couldn't go in to see the band until things were sorted out. Lisa waited for him at the base of the stairs. She drooped against a wall and let her mind wander.

'Here, give us that grass,' Quentin hissed. He was standing pressed close to her and he slipped his hand into her pocket.

Lisa didn't want an argument but she couldn't

59

understand what was going on. 'Why?' She held on to the tin through the thin wool of her coat.

'Just give it, I'll explain later,' Quentin said in such a stern tone that Lisa let her hand go limp. She watched him as he walked back to the bouncer and handed over her tin. She thought she saw a swagger that had not been there before in his retreating shoulders.

'Don't sulk.' Quentin squeezed her hand. 'I'll get you something much better than that.'

'And my tin?'

'Fuck that.'

Lisa felt the words kick in her stomach. It was as if something ugly had been poured down her throat. She wrenched her hand away and crossed her arms underneath her coat, digging her nails into the skin below her armpits.

'Lisa, Lisa, sweetheart.' Quentin pressed her back against the damp wall of the basement. 'Don't be like that, you'll break my heart.'

Lisa knew she should leave, get out, go home, but she felt so tired suddenly and drunk, and her head was full of filings. It was easier to believe what he was saying. 'Lisa, darling,' he murmured as she gave in to him, and with a long sigh, as if he had risked losing something precious, he buried his head in her neck.

Quentin and Lisa stumbled out on to the street. It was midnight. Lisa felt as if days or even weeks had passed since one o'clock at King's Cross station.

Quentin wanted her to come home with him.

'I can't,' she said, 'my mother will be worried.'

Quentin looked puzzled and then a little angry. Lisa hadn't mentioned she lived with her mother. 'Phone her. Tell her you're staying over with a friend.'

60

'I can't,' Lisa said miserably, 'we don't have a phone.'
She felt hollow with cigarette smoke and the heel of her
shoe was squeaking like a taxi. She wanted Quentin to
kiss her and ask when he could see her again.

'Come home with me,' he demanded.

They had walked the length of Upper Street. If Lisa left
him now, she could get the last tube home from the Angel.

'I could see you tomorrow?' she ventured.

Quentin didn't speak. The heat had gone out of his
hand. He didn't want to see her tomorrow, she knew
that. He walked with her into the tube station and they
travelled down in silence in the lift.

'Watcha, Quent,' someone called as they walked out
on to the narrow platform. It was the actor from *Scum*.
The boy who'd been raped. In spite of herself Lisa was
relieved to see him alive and looking so cheerful.

'Got any drugs?' The actor nudged Quentin, and then
winked and said, 'Nah, only joking.'

The actor was on his way to a party. 'Why don't you
come?' And Lisa and Quentin, seeing a way of postpon-
ing their differences, took him up on his offer.

Lisa wouldn't have missed this party for the world. It
was one thing to have met her first real-life actor, but the
party was full of them. There was the main bully from
Scum and the star of *Quadrophenia*. *Quadrophenia* was the
first film Lisa had seen when she arrived in London and
she had even toyed with the idea of writing a fan letter
to the boy who played Jimmy. She could see him now,
fooling about on the dance floor. Thank God, Lisa
thought. Thank God I didn't write.

Quentin didn't want to dance. Lisa was so excited she
couldn't sit still and she left him sitting alone on a row of
chairs. Lisa wasn't a natural dancer. 'Just listen to the

61

bass,' Ruby had told her when she asked for advice, but hard as she tried, Lisa was never sure she knew which one it was.

After three or four self-conscious numbers Lisa went back to find Quentin. He was sitting in the same chair, bent double and sobbing into his hands.

Lisa had never seen a man cry before. She assumed it must be something she'd done. Inadvertently dancing too close to someone on the dance floor or refusing to go home with him. 'I'm sorry.' She was secretly thrilled with the implications of his distress. 'I'm sorry.' She forgave him everything. For stealing her grass and refusing to explain, and not letting her go home when she wanted to. 'Don't cry,' she said and she put her arms around him and kissed the salty side of his face.

Quentin took a long time to come round. His sobs subsided and, just when he'd stopped and shaken his shoulders and taken some air into his lungs, his face collapsed again and he buried his head in his hands. 'Amanda,' he moaned with such despair that it took Lisa a moment to register the other name.

Lisa felt like a fool. Twelve hours with Quentin had wiped her thoughts clean of anyone but him, and she found it hard to accept that all the time Amanda, Amanda, Amanda had been beating in his blood.

Lisa choked back her pride and listened. Amanda was Quentin's girlfriend. They had been living together for over a year and then she had gone to America for the summer to visit a friend. She had written at first and then the letters stopped and there was a long silence in which Quentin convinced himself things couldn't be as bad as they appeared. Eventually he learnt the truth. Amanda wasn't coming back. She was engaged to a

Wyoming rancher and they were to be married on Christmas Eve. By the end of this story Quentin was lying with his face in her lap and his arms wrapped around her knees. He was sobbing like a child. Lisa thought she could see people looking over at them as the party began to thin out.

'Come on,' she said tenderly, prising him up, 'let's go home.'

Lisa couldn't find her key. She had to bang on the door for some time before her mother's sleepy footsteps could be heard shuffling over the floorboards.

Marguerite stood there in her nightdress and looked from Quentin to Lisa. 'I thought when you didn't come home, you must have decided to stay the night with a friend,' she said, and Lisa wondered if she'd ever be able to forgive her.

Marguerite shut the door behind them. She didn't comment on Quentin's presence, or introduce herself, but informed them in a matter-of-fact voice, 'It's three-thirty in the morning,' and went back to bed.

Lisa picked Max up like a Christmas lamb and carried him through to the sitting-room, tucking him into her empty bed, without interrupting one long murmur of his dream. Lisa made herself and Quentin mugs of tea with three sugars each and they climbed into the iron bunk in the bathroom. 'Where else am I going to go?' she whispered, when Quentin mouthed that Lisa's mother was lying on the other side of the thin wall, and she turned her face away from him and let her limbs dissolve into an ashen sleep.

'It must be weeks since I saw or heard of Ruby,' Marguerite said. It was Monday morning and Lisa was leaving for college. She had the door half open. 'Have you seen her?'

'No. Not really.'

'What do you mean, "Not really"?'

'Mum . . .' Lisa protested. Her mother had a habit of introducing new and important subjects just as she was about to leave the house. Sometimes Lisa thought that all their most memorable conversations had taken place with a half-closed door between them.

'Well, you must know where she is living?' Marguerite insisted. Lisa began to edge her way out. She mumbled something unintelligible, even to herself.

'Wait!' Marguerite shrieked, as Lisa inched out of the door. The force of her voice swung Lisa back into the room and just in time to see Marguerite smash her breakfast bowl into the sink. 'Why will no one ever tell me what's going on?' she roared.

Lisa closed the door gently and leant against it, hoping to soak up at least some of her mother's fury.

'I'm sick to death of it,' she screamed, and Lisa hated herself for standing frozen and unable to answer, with only the torments of the arched ears of their neighbours listening in her mind. 'I'm bloody sick to death of it all.' Her mother's voice caved in and her mouth quivered with a rush of tears as she leant over the sink to pick the bits of china from the washing-up.

64

'Oh Mum, darling . . . please don't cry.' Lisa put her arms around her. 'I'll find Ruby, I promise.'

'It's just that no one ever tells me what's going on.' She was sailing now on a noisy rush of sobs. Lisa stroked her hair. She glanced at the clock. She was going to be late. She longed for the anonymity of the long grey corridors of her college.

'Mum, I've got to go,' and she untwined her arms and went to get a towel to dry her mother's face.

Max was still in his pyjamas. He had made a camp under his bed and was only visible from the knees down. He had started school the week before at a nursery on the other side of Bath Street, where he insisted on wearing his plumed plastic helmet with the visor up. Without it, nothing could entice him through the gates.

'Mum,' Lisa said coaxingly, 'hasn't Max got to be at school in a minute?' and, feeling that she had done everything in her power, she ran at full speed down the ramp between the tower blocks, taking the short cut to the station.

Dear Dad, Lisa wrote in her afternoon tea break. *Maybe me, you, and Ruby could have supper one night? College is going fine. Home life is a bit hellish.* (She felt guilty saying this, but she knew how he loved a hint of intrigue and she hoped to hasten his reply.) *Will you let me know: 52 Peerless Flats. EC1. I hope you're well. Lots of Love, Lisa.*

His reply came by return of post. *Meet me at the Greek at 11.30 next Tuesday eve. I'll try and track down Ruby. Hope those hell gates aren't closing in. Might have a plan. Dad.*

Lisa was so thrilled by this note, written on the back of

65

a betting slip, that she locked it in her treasure chest with her other most precious belongings. Lisa's treasure chest was a wooden box she'd been given for her fourth birthday and was one of the few possessions that had been retained from so many moves and burglaries and changes of address. Apart from her father's letter the most recent addition was a square of lined paper with an address written on it in Quentin's sure hand: 111 Crouch Hill. She silently regretted the ugliness of the word 'crouch'.

Lisa and Quentin had been woken the following morning by Max shouting into Quentin's ear, 'Foxes alarm. Foxes alarm.' Quentin had rolled over and tried burying his head in the covers, but Max wanted a fight. He scrambled down to the end of the bed and bit Quentin's toes and chanted: 'Mr Fox has lost his sox. Mr Fox is stoooopid,' until Quentin did what Max wanted and wrestled with him on the floor of the bathroom. He held him upside down by his feet until he laughed so hard his eyes shone like apple pips and he wriggled out of his trousers.

Quentin dressed while attempting to stave off Max's running assaults. Max used his head as a battering-ram and his arms and legs as creepers. He clung on to Quentin just above the knee and let himself be dragged along like a duster. Lisa watched from the bed as Quentin tore a sheet of paper from a notebook in his jacket pocket, wrote on it, and handed it to her.

'Will I see you next weekend?' he said, as he tried to shake himself free. Lisa felt too sad to answer.

'Goodbye,' she heard her mother's voice drift out from the kitchen as Quentin stood by the front door grappling with Max in an increasingly desperate attempt to extricate himself.

'Goodbye,' he mumbled and Lisa saw him blush a deep crimson just a minute before he freed himself and slipped away.

The Greek was a Greek restaurant in Bayswater. Lisa had been there once before. She had got so drunk on the retsina they served that she had walked into the toilet door and nearly knocked herself out.

Lisa didn't want to be the first to arrive. She wandered in and out of the twenty-four-hour shops on Queensway to gain some time. She flicked through rows of Oxford University T-shirts, and glanced at the postcard tiers of naked women and the Union Jack, avoiding the eyes of the Arab men who watched her with suspicious smiles.

Fashionably late was what Lisa hoped she'd be when she walked into the candlelit basement of the restaurant at nearly quarter to twelve, but neither Ruby nor her father was there. Lisa kept her coat on and waited. She ordered a straight vodka and lit a cigarette, but as she sat waiting at the corner table she was plunged so deep into a quicksand of self-consciousness she found she could hardly lift her hand up to her mouth.

Ruby arrived. 'Dad's just coming.'

'How do you know?' Lisa asked, and Ruby slid her a scowl of incomprehension. 'Because we came together. By taxi.'

Lisa pulled hard on her cigarette to drown out the ringing in her ears. Her mother had once told her that she'd hit a woman for implying that the baby she was carrying, Lisa, unborn, was not her father's child. She didn't have to be told that she was not the only one to suspect it. She wondered if Marguerite had hit her father too. She could see her mother's beautiful freckled arms flailing and her hair sticking to her face as she cried through her nose.

'Hello, Dad,' Lisa said, as her father slid into the seat beside her and kissed her very lightly on the side of the head. They ordered Greek salad with squares of feta cheese, and spinach in pastry, spicy sausage, olives and artichoke hearts just to start.

Lisa told Ruby and her father about life in Peerless Flats. She told them about Max wanting to go out and play as if they still lived in the country, and how he charged round and round the concrete yard of the tower block encased in his suit of armour. Ruby and her father both laughed and Lisa warmed up so much she was able to take off her coat. She told them about Marguerite's campaign for a bigger flat and the regular Monday morning battles with the caretaker.

'I was thinking,' her father said, 'I might be able to get you somewhere else to live.'

Lisa wasn't sure. After all she was the reason her mother had moved to London. She wasn't sure she could desert her.

'It might be easier for them as well,' Ruby said, sensing her uncertainty.

'What sort of thing?' she asked her father.

'I don't know. I'd ask around. Maybe a room in a house. A family I know . . . somewhere central.'

Lisa's mind swelled with images of white terraces and the polished steps of double front doors. She imagined herself wandering through a mahogany-panelled drawing-room into a bedroom with a dressing-table and muslin curtains that swelled in the breeze. Then she remembered Max, and his half-bunk in the bathroom.

'I'll see if I can last out,' she said, and she heaped her plate with warm bread and salad, and glanced up at her father to see if he would forgive her the rejection.

Ruby was in a bad mood. She tried to hide it from her father but she let Lisa know with every stab of her fork. She had abandoned her cockney accent for this evening, but when their father left the table to talk to one of the waitresses, she reverted back. 'I've been seein' loads of that bastard Tom. In fact a bit too bleedin' much of 'im.'

'But I thought Tom was —'

'Yeah, I know, but he bloody moved to London, didn't he?'

'Is he staying with Sarah?' Lisa asked, wondering why Sarah hadn't mentioned it. Her heart was pounding in uncomfortable stony beats.

'Nah.' Ruby leant over the table to spike a slice of squid. 'He's got a flat in Mayfair.'

'Mayfair!'

'Yeah, he bloody said I could stay there with him, and then when I moved in, it turned out he meant: stay there *with* him. Literally.'

'What do you mean?' Lisa's hands were trembling.

Ruby looked at her and dropped the cockney. 'Oh, I don't know. He's insisting I sleep in his bed, or he's going to throw me out.'

'Have you not got anywhere else to go?' Lisa was trying to be helpful. 'What about Jimmy?'

'Fuck Jimmy,' but before Ruby could go on, their father returned, sliding into his seat between them.

Lisa wondered momentarily why Ruby didn't ask about Dad's family. The ones with a spare room in their central London house, but she knew why. Ruby wasn't the family type. It was then that she remembered her mother and the reason why she'd asked for supper. She waited until they were out on the street.

'Mum's worried about you,' Lisa said to her as they watched their father disappear in his taxi.

'Really?' Ruby sounded unconvinced.

'Why don't you come round sometime? It's not that bad really.'

'Yeah, I will.'

'Please do,' Lisa pleaded. Ruby shuffled her feet furiously before giving in with a promise. They shared a taxi, stopping first at Mayfair.

'Do you want to come in?' Ruby asked. They were in one of those tiny streets still covered in cobbles where the garages were all converted stables. Lisa looked up at the window with its white light and shook her head. Ruby hugged her. 'Me lil' sis,' she said affectionately. 'I'll see ya soon.'

Lisa watched her as the taxi bumped away. She could hear her calling up at Tom's window. 'Let me in, you bastard, I've lost me bloody key.' She was still standing there when the taxi turned out of the mews and headed east.

Lisa went to the pub to look for Quentin on both Friday and Saturday night. She squeezed her way through the crowds, hovered at the bar, and even went down into the basement to see if he was listening to the band. Quentin seemed to have disappeared. She plucked up courage and asked the bouncer if he'd seen him. The bouncer looked down at her and kissed his lips together. He made a sound like a little bird. Lisa waited, but that was all he seemed prepared to say.

Lisa walked home along the high street. She walked fast with a fixed smile on her lips and a preoccupied air as if she were reliving the events of a wonderfully entertaining evening. She had an uneasy feeling she was being watched. When she had to pass the crowd milling about outside the late-night cinema, she was so certain she saw Quentin's brown eyes staring out at her that for a moment she even thought she heard his voice. 'Lisa,' her name rang out, 'Lisa, Lisa,' and, convinced it was the hissing of her own ears, she began to run. She ran with her heart pounding 'Lisa' in her mouth, and as she clattered down the street her name ran with her like a snake. She ran so fast she felt sick and then her weak heel gave way and cracked right off and she was grounded. This time she didn't care. She bent down to slip off the broken shoe and sling it into the gutter. I'll walk home barefoot, she thought, and then the echo of her name caught up with her and an arm slipped around her waist, raising her up from the pavement.

'You can run but you can't hide,' Quentin said in his velvet voice, and with his hand on her shoulder he limped her back towards the cinema.

Lisa didn't like to mention that it was Quentin who seemed to have been hiding. She struggled with a tangled rope of explanations as to why she might have been fleeing demons the length of Upper Street, alone on a Saturday night, and with only one good shoe, but Quentin showed no signs of curiosity. He rejoined the queue and they inched their way forward in silence. Lisa's palm sweated as she tussled with the starts of conversations. She sneaked a look at him. He stood calm and comfortable, his profile perfect and at ease. 'Quentin, what are you thinking?'

Quentin looked at her. He let go of her hand. 'I don't know,' he said, stepping away. 'What are you asking for?'

'I don't know,' Lisa backtracked. He had pulled away from her as if she were a spy, as if by putting her mind to it she could see into his head.

'I was just wondering how you'd been all week,' Lisa tried to save herself, and then with a flicker of rebellion she added, 'I mean, how do you know I even want to see a Marlon Brando triple bill?'

'Well, don't you?' he asked, and Lisa, balancing on one shoe, weighed up the chances of losing him again and sullenly agreed. They sat through *A Streetcar Named Desire* and got about half an hour into *Last Tango in Paris* when Quentin squeezed her hand and said, 'Let's go, I'm knackered.'

Quentin hailed a taxi. '111 Crouch Hill,' he ordered as he held the door for Lisa. There was no discussion and no pause for one. Lisa sat huddled in Quentin's embrace

73

as they climbed higher into the rises of north London. She thought about her mother and how she'd destroyed, one by one, the last excuses of her childhood.

Quentin was disgusted. 'You're not a virgin, are you?'

'No,' Lisa said. 'Of course not.' A high note of outrage made her voice break like a boy's. 'I'm just not in the mood, that's all.'

They lay coldly side by side on Quentin's thin mattress. Lisa could hear Quentin's flat-mate, Paul, giggling and talking through the wall. He had a girl in his room. Paul was a dealer too. He had looked her up and down when they were introduced and something in his look had said, 'You won't last long,' but with sympathy. Lisa thought bitterly of Amanda.

Quentin sighed and snorted. 'If you're going to be like that,' he said, 'at least you can give me a wank.'

Lisa froze with the shame of it.

It's not that I'm a prude, she thought desperately to herself. In her last year at school, a 'prude' and 'frigid' were the worst things you could be. She just wished it could be different. Lisa knew that he was waiting and she reached out and placed her hand on the flat of his belly. He groaned. He was faking. It couldn't be nice. There was too much disgust and uncertainty in her touch. She moved her hand tentatively across his skin and before he could fool her with another moan she drew it quickly away.

Quentin leapt from the bed, pulling the blanket roughly so that she had to cling on to a sheet to keep from being uncovered. He stood naked and angry in the moonlight. She knelt up in her iceberg sheet and watched his erection droop and wither, shrinking into its shell. 'I'm sorry,' she said.

Lisa tried to cry her way out. She pushed her face into the pillow and prayed for the slippery relief of tears. Her eyes were as dry as glass. Even her bones had lost the juice of their marrow and they clicked and cracked when she moved. She felt as dry and brittle as burnt-out coal. When she looked up, Quentin had left the room.

Lisa had a bath the next morning in Quentin's bathroom. She took off her ring, and searched for stray grips in the remains of her hairstyle.

Lisa had woken determined to take Amanda's place. She had peered at the sleeping beauty of Quentin's high forehead and the sweep of his black lashes. She had rested her head on the cushion of his shoulder and hoped he would wake up. She made two cups of tea and brought them back to bed. 'Quent,' she whispered. 'Sweetheart.' She used his own words to lure him. Quentin flung out his arm, just missing her nose, and buried his head in the covers.

Lisa lay in the bath and pondered over strategies. She accepted she would have to sleep with him. Properly. It wouldn't be so bad. She'd done it before and it was never as bad as she made out. She dreaded the shakes it gave her. It made her body jolt uncontrollably like an epileptic. Between each muscle spasm she thought she might die of embarrassment. All she wanted was for him to hold her hand again as if they were the only two people in the world.

Lisa waited so long for Quentin to wake up that she began to feel restless. She helped herself to a bowl of

Sugar Puffs in the kitchen and was unable to resist glancing through the various possessions strewn around the room. She came across a photograph of Amanda. She knew it was Amanda because it made her stomach spin. Amanda was beautiful. She had long golden curls and heavy-lidded eyes. She was wearing blue jeans and a soft, yellow padded jacket, and she was leaning against a table as if she had just come in from outside. From tennis or riding. Amanda was not the kind of girl you picked up in a pub. Amanda was the girl at school all the boys wanted to marry.

Lisa found her coat in a heap by the door and her shoes, which were hardly worth bothering with, under a cushion. She was tempted to leave them as a grim reminder for Quentin when he woke, but she couldn't quite bring herself to part with them, and so with her hair still wet, and her feet bare, she tiptoed down the stairs and out into the autumn quiet of Crouch Hill. The moment she slammed the door she remembered her ring in its own pool of water lying on the edge of the bath.

When Lisa arrived home, after a bus journey, a series of ill-chosen trains and the long way round from the station for fear of broken glass, it was early afternoon and Ruby had arrived. She sat at the kitchen table picking nuts and raisins, dry, out of a bowl of muesli. Marguerite sat opposite her with Max on her lap. She glanced up as Lisa came in. 'Where've you been?' Her voice didn't carry the weight of worry Lisa had hoped it would.

'Oh you know . . .' Lisa began.

'Yeah Mum, don't be nosy,' Ruby said, pulling Lisa down on to the edge of her chair.

Ruby had changed colour. The skin on her face was yellow, like an egg hard-boiled in onion, and, as Ruby lifted her head out of her bowl of cereal to squint disapproval at her mother, Lisa could see that she had lost the whites of her eyes.

Lisa glanced startled up at Marguerite. Marguerite was leaning over Max. 'Are you going to help me make pancakes?' she asked. Max hung shyly round her neck and whispered that he would.

Ruby bristled at the word 'pancake'. She thrust her bowl away from her and stood up. Lisa wondered that her mother never connected the cause of Ruby's fury with her own haphazard comments. To Ruby, pancakes stood as black as ink for Swan Henderson. Ruby strode up and down the kitchen. She flung open the fridge door and stared into its uninspiring depths. If it wasn't for the loathing that made it impossible for her to say Swan's name, Ruby might have given her reasons for disdaining to stay even for the mixing of the batter. Ruby slammed the fridge door too hard to stick, and it lunged out again and hung open on its hinges.

'I'm off,' she said, her back bent under the weight of a black leather jacket.

'Nice jacket,' Marguerite said.

'It's Tom's.' Ruby swore as her hand caught in the ripped lining of a sleeve.

Lisa walked her to the bottom of the stairs. 'Are you all right?'

Ruby looked at her, her pupils pinpoints in an oval dish of yellow. 'Yeah, I'm fine.' And then she added with a wince, 'Don't say anything to Mum.'

*

77

By the time Lisa reclimbed the stairs, Max was already standing up at the table, a tea towel knotted under his arms, stirring busily away at the pancake mix.

'Ruby looked well, I thought?' Marguerite said.

'Ummm.' It was as near as she could get to what her mother wanted to hear. She bent over Max and tried to hug him. 'Get off,' Max whined. Lisa kissed his cheek. 'Yu-uck,' he squirmed. Lisa laughed and hugged him even tighter, only letting go when he started to scream, 'I hate sloppy kisses, I hate sloppy kisses.' Max rubbed his cheek, flicking batter into his eyes.

'Lisa!' her mother said, and Lisa took a last pretend bite out of his dimpled elbow before going through to the bathroom to wash the layers of grime from her feet.

It was nearly two weeks later that Lisa arrived at college to find there was a message for her. The voice teacher, Pete, said she'd have to go up to the head office to collect it. Lisa wanted to know what was in the message and who it was from, but the voice teacher insisted it was confidential. 'Can't you just tell me,' Lisa pleaded, but Pete jutted his chin and said he was only obeying the rules. Lisa stretched her eyes at him. She had been brought up to mistrust anyone who believed in rules.

The head office was on the third floor of the old wing and wasn't open until after lunch. Lisa's fantasies grew with each turn of the stairs. Each flap of swing door brought sweeter and sweeter bids for her and Quentin's reconciliation; each acre of corridor another bend of his knee.

A queue of students waited, wilting up against the wall opposite the door marked 'Head Office'. Lisa joined them. She shuffled her feet and tapped her fingers in a fluttery dance of expectation. She began to imagine her message as a package. A brown-paper package containing her ring and a note with pencil kisses and a time and a place to meet. It occurred to her only a second before she slid through into the dusty light of the office that Quentin had no way of knowing that she was at college, and even if he did, it was unlikely he would know which college she was at.

'Lisa.' The head of department was talking to her. 'Someone has been looking for you.'

79

Lisa's change of heart was so severe it took her breath away.

'A man was here first thing this morning, asking to see you, demanding even, but as we are unable to give out any personal information concerning our students . . .'

'What did he want?' Lisa asked. There was no paper package.

'He wouldn't say exactly. He wanted to know where you were, where you lived, but of course . . .' The head went on to explain the various laws concerning the security of each and every pupil.

Lisa was too busy shaking off her disappointment to hear what he was saying. She closed her eyes and, as she attempted to focus in on any other men she knew, Max's father disassociated himself from the crowd and stormed up into her brain. Swan had changed his mind, turned his boat around, or dived, and was standing now dripping in the traffic of the King's Cross one-way system. In London to reclaim his family and his only son.

'If he returns what would you like me to tell him?' The head of department was leaning over his desk at her. He had a kind face that had fallen, the rings under his eyes spreading down his cheeks in deep concentric circles.

'Could you tell me what he looked like?' Lisa asked tentatively. The man frowned into his papers as if she had misunderstood everything.

'He was, well, rather bad-tempered, and . . . tall.' He looked at Lisa to let her know he had given her more time than was ever his intention.

'If he comes back I'll be in the hall all afternoon,' she said. 'Tell him to try and find me.'

*

Lisa sat on her plastic chair and watched as each member of the Full Time Speech and Drama course performed Stanislavsky's 'An Action and Three Activities'. Stanislavsky, or 'Stan', as Denise the American method teacher called him, had a theory of acting that revolved around 'Actions'. Every single thing you did was an Action. Each Action had an Objective, and each Activity you performed related to that Action. Lisa wanted to believe this, but she knew it couldn't possibly be true. As far as she could see, very little she did related to anything at all.

'Does that mean I walk around all day with an Objective?' she asked.

Denise looked at her, frozen, with an arm raised. 'Do you have an Objective?' Her voice was too quiet for comfort. 'You are asking if you have an Objective? Your objective, my dear, is to be an actress.' She let her arm down slowly as if she had been stung in the armpit by Lisa's lack of ambition. 'That is an objective that should be with you always. Every step you take should ring out, "I am an actress."'

Lisa felt humbled. The eyes of the rest of the class were on her.

Eugene performed his three Activities. He walked through an imaginary door and looked around an imaginary room. He walked over and peered into a mirror on the Fourth Wall. The Fourth Wall was Stanislavsky's term for the thin air that divided the actors from the audience. Lisa imagined that when she was sufficiently trained she would actually be able to see the pictures that hung on this wall and look out through the windows that opened off it. Eugene combed his hair and straightened his collar. One. Lisa counted his Activities off on her fingers. Eugene walked over to a chair and picked up his jacket. He pulled it on and buttoned it. Two. Out of the pocket Eugene pulled a piece of paper. He held it up to the light. It had words printed on it in black. It looked like a theatre ticket. Eugene kissed the ticket and put it neatly back in his pocket. With a last look around the room he walked out again through the imaginary door. As soon as he was out, he bounded back in and beamed at the class. 'My Action was to go to a performance of *Evita*.'

'Good,' Denise said, her arms crossed over her chest. 'Eugene, you did good.'

Lisa waited anxiously for her turn. The nearer it got the louder the crackling in her head became. It sounded to her like the badly connected line of a telephone, and sometimes, in frustration, she rapped at her skull with her knuckles as if it were a faulty receiver. Lisa looked up at the strip-lights that ran along the ceiling of the hall. She felt their white heat burning into her. She had heard Heidi, one of the Rhodesian sisters, talking about a man who tested for allergies. Maybe he would say to her, 'No more tomatoes,' and all her troubles would be over.

'Lisa!' Denise shouted as if the whole class were waiting. 'It's your turn.'

Of all the thousands of Activities that must exist in a normal day Lisa was unable to think of one. She peered desperately into her bag for inspiration and saw Max's silver cap gun lying heavily at the bottom.

Lisa strode confidently into the room of Action. She placed her bag on a chair and walked over to the mirror. She nearly crossed her eyes in an attempt to catch a glimpse of her own reflection as she smoothed her hair

and took a good long look at herself. One. Lisa rummaged in her bag. She took out a pencil and a piece of
paper and scribbled down a note. She didn't write proper
words, just made marks on the paper. Lisa folded her
note and placed it on the table. Two. She was so pleased
with herself she had to stop herself from smiling. Lisa
drew the gun out of her bag, raised it to her temple and
pulled the trigger. It made a surprisingly loud noise. Lisa
fell to the ground and lay still and crumpled for a
moment to monitor the effect. There was a cold silence
and then the double doors at the end of the hall creaked.
Lisa opened one eye and saw Tom craning his neck into
the room. He caught sight of her and waved. Lisa stood
up, blushing wildly. She looked hopefully at Denise.
Denise's face was set against her. 'You are mocking the
reality of this situation,' she said. Lisa glanced along the
row of students. They were sniggering into their hands.

The door screeched as Tom attempted to slip unnoticed into the room. Lisa kept her eyes on the ground.

'I am appalled.' Denise sauntered over to the table
and picked up Lisa's suicide note. She smirked as she
glanced over it. 'You see what I'm saying?' And she held
it up to illustrate her point.

Tom coughed.

Lisa reeled at the thought that he might come to her
rescue and present himself as her theatrical agent, whisk-
ing her away in a flurry of abuse, but he stood pale and
willowy by the door and waited until Lisa plucked up
the courage to excuse herself.

'What are you doing here?' Lisa could hardly look at
him.

'It's Ruby . . .' And Lisa realized she must have known

it was Ruby all along. She kept her eyes fixed on his shoes. They were blue and ridiculously long. 'She's in hospital.'

Lisa grinned. Just don't step on my blue suede shoes, her brain hummed all by itself. She's in hospital, in hospital. Lisa always grinned when something terrible happened. She hated herself for it. She had grinned when a friend of her mother's was found hanging by a rope in the attic. She had grinned solidly for two hours while she waited for her mother to come home so she could pass on the message. She tried to force Tom's words through her smile as she sang along to Elvis.

'In hospital . . .'

'She wants to see you.'

The smile on her lips dropped of its own accord and for the first time since Tom croaked his way into the hall, Lisa believed there was a chance Ruby might still be alive.

'She wants to see you,' Tom said again, and he began to lope off down the corridor.

'Tom, Tom, wait for me.' Lisa ran after him and she grabbed hold of his hand. He leant down to kiss her cheek. His breath smelt of hangovers and lunchtime Guinness, and something in Lisa rose up to meet his kiss with a surge of loneliness. For a moment she thought how, if Ruby did die, she and Tom would be irrevocably united in their grief, they would get married as planned, have their three children, and of course they would call their oldest daughter Ruby.

Lisa slammed down hard on this fantasy. She wanted to punish herself for such sickening thoughts, and in disgust she withdrew her hand from Tom's.

*

84

Ruby lay in a high, starched bed in a ward of the Westminster Hospital. The whiteness of the sheets made her yellow face look almost gold and Lisa had to stifle a pang of envy for the glamour of her thin bronze arm.

'She's cold turkey,' Tom had whispered as they entered the ward, and now, as Lisa sat on a stool by Ruby's bed, she tried to decipher what he meant. Brown bread – dead, Eartha Kitt – shit. She assumed cold turkey must be cockney slang for something, but she couldn't find anything to rhyme with turkey. Murky was all she could come up with. If murky was what Tom meant, Lisa couldn't see why he'd bother to be so mysterious about it.

Ruby had hepatitis and it was the hepatitis that was making her yellow.

'But how did you get it?' Lisa asked, wondering if cold turkey meant contagious.

'Dunno. Dirty gear.' And then, too exhausted to keep up the accent, she whispered in her old voice, 'Do I look awful?'

'No, not at all,' Lisa reassured her. 'Not at all.'

'Does Mum know?'

Lisa frowned slightly at what she knew was coming. 'Not yet.' She was determined to withhold a promise, and Ruby, as if sensing the barricade of her decision, didn't press her. There were flowers by the bed and three bottles of Perrier water. Lisa wondered if her father had already been and gone.

'When did you come in?' Lisa asked.

'Last night.' Ruby rattled out a laugh. 'What happened was that I decided to have an early night for once in my life. When Tom came home he saw me passed out, thought I'd overdosed, and called an ambulance. The next thing I know they're pumping out my stomach.'

85

Tom got up from his chair on the other side of the bed and walked down to the end of the ward. Lisa looked at the smile on Ruby's exhausted face. She wanted to believe her.

'Anyway, it was lucky really. They said if I hadn't come in, sooner or later I'd have . . .' Ruby's voice strangled up and caught. She slid down the bed so that only her eyelids were visible over the turn of the sheet. Fat, pearly tears oozed out from under them and slid down the side of her face and into her ear. 'I didn't even know I was ill, I mean I knew I was a bit off colour . . .' She tried to laugh, and Lisa pressed the bone of where she hoped her shoulder was.

Before Lisa left, Ruby made her lean close in to the bed so she could whisper in her ear. 'Listen, I've got a favour to ask.'

Lisa nodded.

Ruby gathered up her strength and curled her lip for a London accent. 'Tom's gone all bleedin' holy on me' – she paused while a nurse trundled by – 'and I've got to get hold of some drugs, bad like.' She pinned Lisa with her eye to instil in her the gravity of the situation. 'Just get a bit of smack for me, and I'll never forget it, promise.'

Ruby pulled some money out of her bedside drawer and handed it over. Two twenty-pound notes, crisp and lying in wait. 'Jimmy'll know where to score. He hangs out Thursdays at the Pied Bull.'

Lisa clutched the money. She wished she could ask her to write it all down.

'Oh, and if Jimmy happens to ask,' Ruby added casually, too casually, 'you can mention where I am.'

Lisa hovered at the end of the ward to see if Tom

86

would say his goodbyes and follow her, but as she watched, he stretched himself across the foot of Ruby's bed and showed no sign of moving. The ward sister pushed past her and bore down on him with short, sharp steps.

Lisa intended to tell her mother about Ruby as soon as she got home. She imagined her, furious at not having been the first to know, railing round the kitchen. She saw her elbows shivering on the metal of the draining-board as she cried with her head in her hands. Lisa put off telling her for so long that to come out with the news now, all of a sudden, would be suspicious and inexcusable.

Lisa was distracted for a short time by the conversation over supper. It was dominated by Max. Max described in detail a drawing he had done that day at school. It was a drawing of a fox and he had spent all morning on it. He had made it as big as it would go with zigzag, pointy teeth and a tail that curled up to the roof of the page. Max recreated the shape of it with the pronged end of his fork. Shortly after finishing his picture, just minutes away from home time, another boy, a boy Max hated anyway called Nermil, had taken the fox and, creasing it into a paper aeroplane, had sailed it out of the window and into a puddle. There was nothing Lisa or Marguerite could say to abate his fury. He stabbed at Nermil's name with his fork. He said Nermil was really a gerbil in disguise. He said he was going to kill him.

Lisa ran her fingers through his hair and offered to read him a story. Max flung her hand away and scowled, and then an instant later, sensing his mistake, he crawled on to her lap and said, 'All right, as long as it's a comic.'

Lisa hated comics and Max knew it.

'You're not reading it properly!' he complained every time she missed a bubble or a sound effect.

'Sorry. "Thwack. Splat." Better?'

She kept flicking through to see how far it was to the end.

'Don't do that, it's not fair,' Max whined.

'Lisa!' her mother called through from the washing-up.

Lisa knew the only way out was to start again. 'I'm just going to the phone box,' she called when she had finished, and she slipped out on to the stairs.

Lisa walked up and down Peerless Street. There was a pub at one end into which she was curious to go. She peered through the bottle-base panes of its windows but could see no customers, only a blur of red plush and bar stools and the tottering reflection of the tower blocks. In all those hundreds of flats, she thought, looking up, there must be someone I could get to know.

She was about to turn back into her staircase when Steen appeared as if from nowhere and put his hand on her shoulder. 'How're you doing?'

Lisa hadn't noticed it before, but he was dressed from head to toe in shades of faded orange.

'Fine.' And then she remembered and added, 'Thanks again for that grass.'

Steen stood and stared at her with his eyes moist and bulging. Lisa couldn't think of anything else to say. 'Do you know where the Pied Bull is?' she asked to break the intensity of his gaze, even though she knew very well it was at the Angel.

'What's a pied bull?'

Put like that Lisa didn't really know. Then a thought struck her. Maybe she wouldn't have to go to the Pied Bull after all. She remembered Steen's previous generosity and thought how she might not only save herself a bus fare, but be able to keep some of the crisp forty pounds Ruby had given her. 'You don't by any chance,' she asked him, 'have any heroin I could buy off you?'

Steen swayed slightly. 'You must be joking!' He looked genuinely shocked. He closed his eyes for a moment, and then, giving her a final liquid stare, he walked away down the street.

Marguerite looked up at her. She was kneeling by the bath washing Max with a flannel.

'Ruby's got hepatitis. She's in hospital and she'd like it if you'd visit her,' Lisa said almost in a breath.

'What, now?'

'Well it's probably a bit late now.' Lisa felt as if she were towering above her mother. 'Visiting times . . .'

Marguerite was silent.

'Maybe tomorrow?' Lisa suggested.

Marguerite rubbed hard at the dirt around Max's neck, making him shout and wriggle away from her like a tadpole. Lisa leant against the bathroom door. She was waiting for her mother to react, but for once it seemed she had decided against it.

Lisa wandered through to the sitting-room and sat down on her bed. It was getting late. She toyed with the idea of not going to the Pied Bull. She could tell Ruby that Jimmy hadn't been there, or that he had been there but without any drugs, or that the pub had been raided and closed down. It wasn't so much going to the Pied

Bull, but the inevitable conversation with Jimmy Bright that Lisa dreaded. She had never managed to say more than a few words in his presence and even those she had regretted.

'Some of them peas please,' she said now, in an attempt to lose her south-coast voice, and, 'All right, Jim mate? All right?'

Lisa picked up her coat and reached behind her for the handle of the door. 'Listen, I won't be back late,' she mumbled, as if any other details had been previously discussed.

Marguerite looked troubled. 'But don't you have college in the morning, surely?' she asked, knowing she did.

'Yes, but it'll be all right. It's just – look, I'll see you later,' and Lisa wriggled backwards and slipped out on to the stairs.

Marguerite let her go. Lisa knew that her mother regretted the line she had taken with Ruby, ordering her home by eleven, allowing Swan to interrogate her over boyfriends and insisting that she not hitch-hike alone. These attempts at discipline had, she felt, lost her her eldest daughter and, in the wake of Ruby's rebellion, Lisa had inherited a free rein. And anyway, Lisa was sensible. Lisa had been told how sensible she was ever since she could remember. She had even been introduced to people on occasion as the only truly sensible member of her family.

As Lisa walked quickly through the short cut, she thought of Tom and saw his blue shoes hanging off the end of Ruby's bed. In a lazy attempt to push away his image she began to dwell on Quentin, and with a pang she realized she held the perfect excuse for seeing him again. This would not only be her chance for a reconciliation, but she might also be doing him a favour. If he were really as down on his luck as he made out, surely he would appreciate her bringing him some business.

Lisa took the tube to Finsbury Park and waited in the dingy and deserted station for a bus.

'Half, please,' she said, when a bus finally pulled in.

'Half to where, love?' The driver looked at her sceptically.

'Crouch Hill.'

'Yes, Crouch Hill. Crouch Hill where? Top, bottom, halfway up?'

'Halfway up,' Lisa guessed, hoping she wouldn't be thrown off too far from her destination.

'Right, now that we've got that clear.' The driver looked at her. 'How old did you say you were?'

'Thirteen,' Lisa gasped, wide-eyed and with an air of breathy incredulity.

The driver held her stare for a moment and then, whistling through his teeth, punched her out a ticket.

There were three bells by Quentin's front door and Lisa rang them all. No one appeared. She rang them again and waited. As she stood awkwardly on the broken path, she glanced up at his window, slightly open at the top of the house, and saw that a light had been switched on.

That doesn't necessarily mean he's in, she told herself fiercely, arguing against the possibilities. And then, as she watched, she saw a long black shadow sweep across the square of light, move away from the window and vanish. Lisa slunk into the wall, squeezing herself between a row of dustbins, pushing away the thought of Quentin's smile that would settle on his face like a bow as he watched her waiting hopefully. It made the sweat

91

stand out cold on her back. She crept around the side of the house, scrambled out through the hedge, and streaked away over the brow of the hill. The same bus stopped for her on its return journey.

'Finsbury Park,' she said woefully, unable to catch the driver's eye, and he punched her out a half fare anyway.

It was nearly closing time when Lisa walked into the Pied Bull. She clung desperately to the importance of her mission as she had first experienced it. She thought of the fix of Ruby's yellow eye, and the enormity of her task.

Lisa nestled her toes against the edges of her twenty-pound notes, folded for safety one each in the soles of her shoes. The pub was almost empty. She looked around for Jimmy, half hoping not to find him, but he was there, lounging against the jukebox. Lisa walked purposefully over to him.

'Jimmy?' Her voice came out unexpectedly in a high squeak. Jimmy flashed round on her, and for a moment, just before his face softened, she saw the tip of what Ruby had warned her of. His scornful, razor-sharp tongue.

'Watcha, lil' sis,' he said with a laugh. 'Got a message for me, have you?'

Lisa nodded.

'How is she, then, Ruby, the jewel of my life?' Jimmy tapped his foot and broke into a country-and-western croon, 'Oh Ru-ubeey, don't take your love to town.'

Lisa edged a little nearer to him. 'She said you'd be able to sell me —'

'Yeah yeah, all right, great.' Jimmy cut her off, and he

clicked his finger at the barman and ordered her a bottle of Pils. 'Right,' Jimmy hissed into her ear. 'Give us the money.' Lisa stared down at her shoes. Jimmy looked away and sighed a low, hopeless sigh, and Lisa, refusing to be given up on, dropped her bag and, on bending down to retrieve it, slipped her fingers into her shoes and came up triumphantly with the notes.

'All right, drink this, and wait here,' Jimmy said, pushing her glass towards her, and he disappeared through the side door of the pub. Lisa felt a fog settle down over her head. Her left ear hummed as if it had been topped up with water. She stared miserably into the pale round of her beer, scanning its surface for a trace of what she feared, and resolving not to take the risk of drinking it.

It was eleven-fifteen. Lisa took a sip of Pils from the sheer boredom of waiting. At any minute, she thought, the pub would close. She supposed she would have to wait for Jimmy out on the street, and then it occurred to her for the first time that he might not come back. She took a long gulp of lager and regretted it. Now she would not only be waiting for Jimmy but also for the possible disintegration of her brain. She had just condemned herself to twenty minutes of torture, if not a lifetime in a lunatic asylum. She considered ordering an orange juice – Lisa had once been told that the vitamin C in orange juice worked against the hallucinogenic effects of acid – but she decided against it. If her drink was spiked, it would have been the barman, possibly on Jimmy's orders, who had spiked it, and therefore he would be bound to know what she was up to. Apart from anything else acid was expensive and he wasn't likely to let her waste the effects of a good tab. Lisa had another theory that stopped her from ordering orange juice. She was certain that for an under-age drinker to ask for a soft drink would be a sure way to arouse suspicion and bring up the question of whether she should actually be in a pub in the first place.

It was nearly twelve and the Pied Bull showed no sign of closing. Lisa began to worry about her mother. She imagined her waiting up. Listening for every tread on the stairs. She knew from experience that the more she worried about her mother, the less anxious her mother seemed when she did finally appear. But it didn't stop her. Maybe this was what people meant by sensible.

Lisa hovered by the bar, her eyes fixed on the door in an agony of indecision. I'll wait five more minutes, she told herself regularly, and then another five, and the first five after that. She talked herself in and out of giving up on Jimmy, abandoning the money, declaring his treachery to Ruby. But it was at this point in her revolving thoughts that she submerged into the deathbed scene. She saw Ruby's yellow hand reach out to her, pleading for a sign of Jimmy Bright's devotion, her dry lips moving wordlessly, her eyes alight with fever, she saw Ruby sink into the hospital pillow, Ruby, too weak to speak.

Lisa shook herself. She looked up at the clock, into the froth of her empty glass, and around the room at the few remaining people. She glanced, minutely hopeful, towards the door, and with a shock like a punch she saw that it was bolted. She felt herself freezing. Her knees lost their joints and her head shrunk to the size of a tennis ball. The thought of the side door whirred in the pit of her stomach. It loomed larger than life as her only real means of escape. She pulled herself around, expecting to find it vanished, to find the door bricked up or disguised in some way by a row of jukeboxes or a revolving bookcase, but it was still there, unlocked and unmanned, and as she grappled with her dissolving knees, it swung open, and Jimmy Bright strode in.

'Jimmy!' Lisa stumbled towards him.

Jimmy narrowed his eyes. He tilted his head, and motioned for her to follow him outside.

The wind was up and howling round the Angel. They rushed along, their elbows out to fight off the sheets of plastic and the flying cardboard boxes. Jimmy, shaking a clinging newspaper from his foot, dodged into a doorway.

Lisa waited for a lull. 'Have you got it?'

Jimmy winced. He turned to face her. 'Listen, girl, it's up to you. You can either come back tomorrow, or we can give the Old Man a try.'

Lisa gulped. 'Let's try the Old Man,' she said, shaken, but thrilled to be given even the most slender of choices, and she followed Jimmy cheerfully as they skidded on through the swirling litter.

The Old Man was a woman. She was tall and thin and looked about twenty-five. She lived in a basement in a large damp room that smelt faintly of gas. No one spoke. Jimmy handed over the money.

The Old Man curled the notes around her finger, modelling them into a purple paper ring. Eventually she stood up, stretched, and left the room. A dog that had been sleeping in the corner woke up briskly, his ears on end, and trotted after her.

'She likes to take a cut,' Jimmy whispered.

The Old Man reappeared with a white paper packet

in a polythene bag, a soup spoon and a syringe. Lisa watched as the Old Man poured powder from the packet into the spoon and melted it over the flame of a candle. When it had melted to a slippery brown treacle, she poured it into the syringe, and, shaking her wrists until her fingers thickened, she pierced a fat vein in the back of her hand. The dog began to bark. The hair along its back stiffened. It snapped and growled and gnashed its teeth at the Old Man.

'Shut up, Hassle.' With her eyes on the needle she smiled a proud half-smile. 'He hates it when I jack up.'

Hassle stretched out his front paws and snarled at the empty syringe. He barked so fiercely that foam bubbled and clung at the corners of his mouth. The Old Man drew the needle out and offered it to Jimmy. Hassle's barking faded to a whine and, with his tail between his legs, he retreated to his basket.

'What time do you finish college?' Marguerite asked Lisa over breakfast.

'Five.'

'I'll meet you at Victoria station at half past and we'll go on to the hospital from there.' Marguerite was planning a visit to Ruby and she expected Lisa to go with her. Lisa would have preferred to have gone alone but Marguerite was insistent.

'All right, but please, please don't be late.' Lisa crept into the sitting-room to pack her bag for college. A notebook, Chekhov's *Three Sisters*, her leotard, and Ruby's small white packet of heroin, which she slipped between the loose lining of her satchel.

Lisa sat in the college canteen over lunch with Janey and Eugene. The chip-making machine had stopped working and a furious meeting hosted by the students' union had just broken up. If chips did not reappear on the menu by the following week, the students' union were threatening to set up a picket. Janey and Eugene sat opposite Lisa with a paper plate and five substitute packets of beef, bacon and cheese-and-onion crisps. Lisa had a plate of tinned ravioli. Tinned ravioli was her current favourite food, eclipsing even a cheeseburger. Lisa hadn't grown up with school dinners. For lunch each day she had eaten Marmite sandwiches crumbled at the bottom of a paper bag, an apple and a handful of dried fruit and sunflower seeds. She had only attended the students' union chip-machine meeting out of curiosity and she had been amazed to see so much distress over chips when there was still ravioli available for one and a half luncheon vouchers.

'Was that your boyfriend that came in yesterday?' Janey asked.

It was the first allusion anyone had made to her unsuccessful attempt to impress the method teacher with suicide. Lisa blushed.

'No,' she said. 'No,' she said again and sighed.

'He looked nice.'

'He's sort of my sister's boyfriend.'

'Oh, I see.' Janey leant in closer for an exchange of confidences. 'My sister's got one of those, or at least she did have until she got pregnant and he scarpered.'

'Did she keep the baby?' Lisa asked, assuming she wouldn't have.

'Yeah, Mum and Dad tried to get her to have an abortion, seeing as she was fifteen and everything, but she said she wanted it.' Janey shrugged. 'Takes all kinds. Different strokes for different folks.'

Lisa nodded.

'Are you a feminist?' Janey asked her.

Lisa, never having given the matter much thought, said she thought she probably was.

'Bloody men!' Janey thumped her fist on the table, and Eugene, feeling left out of the conversation, and having turned the last packet of crisps inside out to catch the crumbs, broke into a heartfelt version of 'Don't cry for me, Argentina'.

*

Marguerite was late. Lisa had known all day that she would be, and now, at a quarter to six, it was just a matter of how late she was going to be.

They had arranged to meet by the cartoon cinema at the end of platform 17. Trains to Sussex ran from platform 17, and London, until very recently, had begun and ended for Lisa with this platform and the exotic pull of the cartoons. Lisa looked at the glass-encased posters of Bugs Bunny and Mickey and Minnie Mouse. She had imagined so often what it would be like to sit inside its plush interior and watch Technicolor films throughout a whole day that she couldn't remember whether she had ever actually been inside or not.

She had once been taken to the cinema by a friend of her father's, a girl called Felicity, who had been sent to meet her off the train one Father's Day when her father couldn't make it. Felicity had asked her what she wanted to do and she had said more than anything else she wanted to go to the cinema. She remembered holding Felicity's hand as they stooped to run past the ticket window and slip unnoticed up the red-carpeted stairs. She remembered creeping and falling over the legs of men as they pushed their way to a free seat. But it couldn't have been the cartoon cinema because the film was about a woman with large breasts and long blonde hair who pulled up her petticoats at every opportunity to prove to people that she was in fact a man. The film hadn't been in English and Lisa remembered the subtitles jumping about on the screen. She also remembered that after ten minutes Felicity said it was boring and they had crept out again. Afterwards they had taken photos of themselves in a black-and-white photo booth, all of which Felicity let her keep, and which still occupied a corner of

99

her treasure box. She wondered now what had happened to Felicity.

'Max, would you like me to take you to the cartoon cinema?' she asked, when her mother finally appeared, breathless and full of excuses.

Max stared up at a larger-than-life Pink Panther.

'Yes, but not now.' Marguerite frowned. 'She doesn't mean now.'

'No, another time.' Lisa reached for his free hand. 'Shall I take you another time?'

'All right,' Max said. And he shot at one of Bugs Bunny's ears with an imaginary bow and arrow as they hurried away.

When Lisa, Marguerite and Max arrived at the Westminster Hospital, they found that Ruby had been moved on. She had been sent to a hospital somewhere near Baker Street that specialized in hepatitis.

'You'll be lucky to get there before visiting's over,' the ward sister warned them.

Lisa clutched her bag. 'Come on, let's hurry.' She headed for the stairs. 'Max, if you wait for the lift, we'll be here all night.'

As Lisa shuffled Max through the revolving doors of the main entrance, she saw a familiar shape blurred between the glass partitions. It was Sarah. Lisa stayed in the wheel of the door and caught her in the foyer.

'Ruby's not here,' she told her.

'It's been ages.' Sarah looked at her, curious. 'How are things?'

'It's just that if we don't hurry, we'll miss the end of visiting time.' Lisa could hardly control her agitation. Max and her mother, having followed her back inside were browsing by the kiosk that sold sweets and newspapers. As she watched, her mother joined a queue of men and women in pyjamas. 'Mum, we really should go . . .' she called.

Sarah looked down at her spray of white carnations. 'I suppose I might as well come with you.'

Sarah was in high spirits. 'What do you think about Tom and Ruby, then?' and she nudged Lisa in the ribs. When Lisa didn't answer, she told her about her cousin Tanya, and how she still hadn't succeeded in losing her virginity. 'No,' Sarah sighed. 'So far no luck. Poor thing.' She looked at Lisa and smiled. Sarah could afford to smile. Sarah had a boyfriend. She had a photograph of him in her wallet that she showed round once they were on the bus.

'He looks very handsome,' Marguerite approved, leaning over to have a look.

'Yes, he does.'

'He looks like wee,' Max hissed from under their seat, giving himself away, as Marguerite was about to pay three full fares.

'And a half,' she added, smiling up at the conductor.

The hospital was behind Lisson Grove. It was white and shaped in parts like a church. It stood in its own garden and made the Westminster, with its solid grey wings, look like a multistorey carpark.

'I'm afraid visiting time is over,' a nurse called out to them as they tried to pass unnoticed through the quiet tiled hall of the main entrance.

'I'm sorry?' Marguerite stopped in her tracks as if unable to believe her ears.

The nurse, patient as a nun, repeated her message.

'But my daughter was only admitted today.' Marguerite strode over to her. 'I think she would appreciate a familiar face, even at this ungodly hour.'

Lisa winced. It had been a mistake to mention God. The nurse's white face hardened. She flicked through her book with quick, decisive fingers.

'Yes, I see. Indeed. Well, you will have to return tomorrow at a more . . . appropriate time.' The nurse shut her book. She was waiting for them to leave.

'Excuse me, Sister.' Sarah lowered her voice in reverence. 'Would it be possible, if it wasn't too inconvenient, for you to take these flowers up to her?'

The nurse softened. She placed a hand on the green stalks of the carnations.

Lisa wondered if she shouldn't ask that her small white package be taken up also. If she had known, she could have had it ready in her hand, or even hidden it among the spray of Sarah's frilly flowers. But now it was too late. It would be impossible to rummage through the lining of her bag without arousing anyone's suspicion. She bit her lip and prayed that Ruby would have the strength to hold out.

Lisa got up early the next morning. She left Marguerite to investigate a one-bedroom flat, which according to Frances was coming free that day on the next staircase, and set off for the hospital.

She found Ruby sitting on a bench in the garden. She was as yellow as ever and seemed to have made some friends. She introduced Lisa to two girls. Marlene, who was West Indian and not yellow but a greenish colour, and a girl called Trish, who was so thin and fragile Lisa wondered that she was able to sit up unaided.

'It's brilliant in here,' Ruby beamed, 'you can get all the gear you want.'

Lisa's face fell. She had Ruby's packet of heroin all ready to present to her.

'You just place an order with Trish's boyfriend and next visiting hour it arrives with the grapes.'

'Oh,' Lisa said.

'Yeah,' Marlene winked, 'we don't half save a lot on syringes.' And the three girls erupted into a fit of giggles. Lisa smiled weakly. She still had a stitch from the last sprint from the station. When they had recovered, Trish and Marlene went off to raid the kitchens. 'There's a whole freezer full of raspberry ripple ice cream.'

'No, ta.' Ruby stayed to talk to Lisa.

'In case I forget' – Lisa took out her packet – 'I'd better give you this.'

Ruby slipped it into the pocket of her dressing-gown without a word. 'Did you see Jimmy?'

Lisa nodded. She tried to keep her face brave.

'Well, what did he say?'

Lisa screwed up her eyes. 'What?'

'What did he say?'

'Nothing.'

'Bastard.' Ruby crossed her arms tight over her chest and scowled. Her wrists stretched out of her hospital gown and revealed the white tissue of the scar that had formed over the self-inflicted gash of the bread knife.

'Jimmy did say' – Lisa spoke slowly as if searching out the memory – ' "Ruby, the jewel of my life." '

Ruby tightened her fists.

'He even sang a song about you.'

There was a pause and then Ruby raised her chin. 'Did he? What? He sang a song? About me?'

'Oh Ru-ubeey, don't take your love to town.' Lisa tried to imitate Jimmy Bright's rock-and-roll quaver.

'Oh that old song.' Ruby tossed her head, but she was unable to control the smile that spread over her face like the light behind a Hallowe'en lantern. 'Oh Ru-ubeey, oh Ru-ubeeey, don't take your love to town.'

Marguerite had managed to secure them a new flat. It was identical to the old one except it had an extra room. She and Max were going to sleep in the bedroom in bunk beds and Lisa was to have the sitting-room all to herself.

Lisa promised she would stay in the flat while her mother went to visit Ruby. Marguerite was terrified it would be taken over by squatters if left vacant for even five minutes.

'Won't you leave Max here with me?' Lisa asked, but Marguerite insisted on taking him with her. 'Ruby never sees her little brother.'

Lisa wondered if it had ever occurred to her that Ruby didn't like children. Max was no exception. When Max was born, Ruby could hardly bring herself to look at him. And now as the years passed, and his resemblance to his father grew, she only ever paid him the slightest and most necessary attention. Lisa, on the other hand, had been so overcome the day they brought Max home that she had given up playing with her dolls. She had donated any doll's clothes that fitted to his tiny wardrobe and the rest had been sent to a jumble sale along with their owners. Max was to have no competition. Soon after, Lisa began to suffer recurring nightmares in which pint-sized Max fell through the window of his bedroom, and Lisa would have to race down the stairs, through the front door and out on to the path to try to catch him before he hit the ground. Lisa always awoke from these dreams convinced they were a sign her brother had been struck down by cot death. She spent a large part of each night holding a mirror in front of his face to check that he was breathing.

Lisa wandered around the empty new flat. The kitchen was covered in the same strangling wallpaper, and the bedroom had squares of lime-green and brown in horizontal stripes. Tulips in boxes. Or tunnels. Lisa found if she looked at them for too long she began to feel dizzy. Only the lavatory was lined in plain woodchip. Lisa sat on the edge of the bath for lack of a chair, and listened to the broken lyrics of a Leonard Cohen song wailing through the floorboards of the flat above.

Ruby stayed at the special hospital week after week. The doctors told her she was not allowed to drink alcohol for at least six months, and she was advised to stay in bed for the best part of the day.

Ruby, Trish and Marlene became firm friends. When Lisa visited, she usually found them in the day-room with their feet up in a cloud of smoke, discussing the latest delivery of drugs. Or when the weather was warm enough, out in the gardens shooting up among the rhododendrons.

Sometimes Lisa bumped into her father arriving with white boxes of cake and mineral water. She told him that they'd moved into a bigger flat and that college was going fine. And he said, 'Ruby does seem to be looking better, don't you think?' Once or twice he and Marguerite passed in the corridor, or one arrived as the other was about to leave. They nodded and made friendly faces at each other, but neither of them ventured to speak.

One Saturday Lisa arrived to find that Trish had died in the night. Ruby sat up straight in her starched bed. Only the palest trace of yellow remained in her face and her hands were bone-white. She clasped them in front of her, digging the nails in so hard they drew blood.

Lisa covered her face with her own hands. She felt sick with dread that she might laugh. She looked out at Ruby through the grille of her fingers.

'I'm sorry.'

She wanted to know the details. To know what had actually happened, but she didn't feel able to ask. She was anxious not to appear morbid.

Lisa sat by Ruby's bed all afternoon. She flicked through magazines and ate some of Ruby's sweets. From time to time she glanced at her sister, sitting sphinx-like against a wall of pillows, staring out through the window on the other side of the ward. Just when visiting time was finally over, Ruby started to itch. She twisted and turned in her bed as if she had fleas.

'He's deserted us,' her eyes were blazing and hateful.

'Who?'

'Trish's bloody boyfriend. You won't see him now for dust.'

'Oh,' Lisa said.

'Listen, on your way out, tell the nurse to bring me a couple of Valium or a sleeping-pill or whatever she can get. Ask the one with the big bum, she's the nicest.'

Lisa kissed Ruby goodbye. 'I'll see you tomorrow,' she said.

*

Family life became easier once they moved into the bigger flat. They painted it entirely white and resigned themselves to staying there for some time. Lisa even fantasized about having a party. She would invite Tom, and Sarah, and possibly even Quentin. Steen and the Rhodesians would be bound to drop in whether they were invited or not. She could invite Janey from college.

Lisa had become quite friendly with Janey. She had even begun to confide in her. At least she had told her about Quentin. She hadn't particularly wanted to talk about Quentin, but she felt something was expected of her in exchange for learning how Janey had lost her virginity on the pier at Blackpool.

'Do you think,' Lisa asked her, 'that I should go round there? Just turn up and say I've come to collect my ring?'

Janey wasn't sure. 'What? Today?'

'Why not?' Lisa felt full, suddenly, of bravado.

Janey looked at her. She looked her up and down like a man. 'Maybe you should go some other time when you . . . you know, you've made a bit more of an effort.'

Lisa's face fell. She knew Janey was right. Her hair was stringy and she had a ladder in her tights, but she resented her lack of confidence. 'I thought you said you were a feminist,' she mumbled, and added, silent and mistaken, If Quentin really loved me it wouldn't matter what I looked like.

Ruby was allowed home. The hospital sent letters to both her mother and father informing them of this, and reiterating that Ruby must rest and abstain from alcohol for a further five months.

'Of course you can come to us,' Marguerite told her. 'It'll be a bit cramped, but we'll manage.'

Ruby rolled her eyes. 'I'd prefer to stay here!'

Marguerite looked to Lisa for support.

'It's all right,' Ruby said, kicking off a slipper. 'Dad's found me somewhere.'

Marguerite smiled away her hurt. 'That's wonderful.'

The hospital would have preferred Ruby to have gone to one or other of her parents but Ruby was eighteen, which meant she was over eighteen, and an adult. Ruby's father had a friend whose uncle had recently died. The uncle had been living in a three-bedroom flat in Belgravia, behind the German embassy. This flat was ready for Ruby to move into whenever she wanted.

'Cor blimey!' Ruby said, 'just look at this gaff.'

Lisa unloaded Ruby's bags from the taxi and carried them up the stairs.

'Bugger, bollocks and balls!' Ruby shouted, dancing from room to room.

'Ruby,' Lisa begged her. 'You're meant to be lying down.'

The flat was fully furnished. It had a sitting-room with twin sofas, and chairs and curtains made from matching chintz. The kitchen was enormous and fully equipped with potato-mashers, gravy boats and a well-stocked linen cupboard. The bedrooms were at the back of the flat. They were small, with high, wide beds and lamp-shades draped in muslin. Each one had a bedside table and a wardrobe. Ruby chose the room with the biggest bed. They didn't mention the uncle. The only sign of his previous existence was a row of smart, black shoes at the back of a cupboard.

Ruby asked her father for a colour television to help her while away the time, and she ordered that the phone be reconnected. After a few luxurious but lonely days she moved Marlene in for company.

Marlene had shaken off the murky pallor of her hepatitis and transformed into a cool, languid beauty of breathtaking sophistication. Marlene had a boyfriend who was out to kill her. She had a photograph of them together that she placed in its silver frame on top of the television, and Ruby, convinced all of a sudden that Jimmy Bright and Tom were both more threatening than they had ever shown themselves to be, made Lisa swear to keep her whereabouts a secret.

When Lisa visited, she had to give the bell three short, coded rings to prove it was her, and then Marlene's almond eyes would appear over the kitchen window-ledge, followed by the sound of her narrow feet treading lightly on the stairs. 'Hello, Lisa?' Her voice came through the locked door, double-checking, before her soft hand turned the key.

Ruby and Marlene only ventured out at night. They didn't begin their preparations until the television closed down, and often it was nearly morning before they were ready to leave the house. Marlene was an expert on makeup. She smoothed Ruby's face with creamy white foundation and patted it with powder that smelt of the secret inside of a handbag. She brushed her curled lashes with mascara until her eyes fluttered like moths, her lips she painted a dark blood-red. Marlene shadowed her own eyes in gold and honey-brown, and outlined her lips in silver. Her fine, high cheekbones she dusted over ivory.

Ruby was no longer a punk. She handed on to Lisa her bondage trousers, her DMs and the Snow White T-shirt with the seven dwarfs. She spent most of the day and night lounging in pyjamas, and when she did get dressed, she wore trailing, see-through layers of crêpe de Chine, and high, strappy heels. When Ruby and Marlene ventured out, it was to travel by taxi to the West End.

Marguerite was beginning to despair of the council. There was a family of five on the top floor of Peerless Flats that had been living there for four years. Their children spent the evenings sniffing glue on the roof and pissing down the stairwell. Frances had had no news of her permanent accommodation, and little Brendan, still unseen by his father, was nearly five months old. Lisa saw less of her now that they were no longer direct neighbours, but whenever she did, she found Frances on the verge of giving up and going back to Ireland.

Heidi, one of the pale, red-haired Rhodesian sisters had fallen in love. She had fallen in love with Steen. Heidi's husband moved out on the morning of the day Steen moved in. It was the beginning of the Christmas holidays and Lisa watched from the square-paned window of her bedroom. She felt the whole block cheer as Heidi ran down to help Steen with his bags, her hair wet and brushed straight over her shoulders and her little ginger baby on her arm.

Lisa hadn't spoken to Steen since the day she had shocked him in the street with her talk of hard drugs. She wondered what it was that had stopped him from telling her mother. For weeks she had expected the storm to break, opening the door each evening on a possible typhoon of recriminations only to find Marguerite filling in job application forms, maintaining the same strained air of calm.

Heidi invited them over for a drink. She had transformed her flat into a home for honeymooning. The sour smell was gone and all the dirty dishes and the milk-encrusted baby clothes had been ousted with her husband. There were flowers on the table and the bay window gleamed with the promise of Christmas. Heidi no longer talked about Rhodesia, about the velds and the sunsets and the flocks of wild flamingos. Her eyes sparkled with the possibility of snow and the chance to show her son the lights on Regent Street. Her sister Pam sat across the room, her mouth a thin line of disappointment. It was no fun being homesick on your own. She tugged her gangly, dark-haired daughter on to her knee and hugged her close.

Marguerite joined a housing co-operative. She insisted both Max and Lisa come with her to the first meeting to prove just how badly in need she was of housing. She declared she wasn't going to spend the rest of her life in a bunk bed on Peerless Street.

'Oh Mum,' Lisa said, overcome with guilt, and a twist of dread at the next inevitable move. 'I'll share with Max. I don't mind.'

'Don't be silly,' Marguerite snapped. 'You're a teenager, you need your own space.'

Lisa knew her mother was thinking of Ruby. She was thinking of Ruby and how she had lost her. Lisa wanted to throw her arms around her mother's neck and tell her that she'd never desert her, never leave home, wherever it was, and she mustn't worry or even think about it.

'Of course I'll come to the meeting,' she agreed instead, and she went to try on some of Ruby's newly cast-off clothes.

The New Swift Housing Co-operative was made up mainly of single women and their children. There were a few bearded men in needlecord who took over as soon as the meeting got started. Minutes sheets were distributed. Lisa ran her eye down the long list which included:

Complaints about Jackie

Why is the roof *still* leaking at 199 Huddleston Road

And eventually:

New members

Lisa felt so bored she thought her eyes might drop out and roll away like marbles. She fidgeted and yawned and, without meaning to, turned her minutes sheet into an abstract piece of origami art. The New Swift emblem was a flying bird, a swift in profile. Lisa was disappointed. She had assumed New Swift meant either New people would be housed Swiftly, or at least they would be provided as soon as possible with Swift New houses. Neither of these things seemed likely. By tea break Lisa had resolved to remain forever homeless rather than attend another meeting.

There was a crèche at one end of the room that had been set up by the Co-op for members' children. On arrival Max had barricaded himself into the Wendy house and was busily building armoured personnel carriers out of Lego. Lisa longed for him to stir up a fight or get his finger caught under the wheels of a Thomas the

Tank Engine so that she would have an excuse to go to his rescue, but he remained uncharacteristically well-behaved.

The meeting was still several items away from 'New members' when it dragged on into its third hour. Lisa looked at her mother who was brightly following a conversation about positive discrimination in short-life housing, and with a whispered excuse slipped away in the direction of the toilets. In an alcove below the stairs she found a payphone, and she dialled Sarah's number.

Lisa's fingers trembled with relief as the connection clicked and her two-pence piece slid through its slot and dropped into the box.

'Hello?' It was Sarah. She was at home.

'Hello, it's Lisa.'

'Lisa!' There was something breathy about Sarah's voice that made Lisa think she'd been crying. 'Where are you?'

'I'm not sure, somewhere very boring on the 27 bus route.'

'Do you want to come over?' 'Can I come over?' they said together, overlapping and embarrassing themselves. They laughed and Lisa thought she heard a sniff.

Sarah lived at the top of a house in a square in Kensington. The house was owned by a very old lady who was, or had been, a friend of Sarah's parents. When Lisa rang the bell, the door was answered by an equally ancient woman with a fierce look and a bent back. She had to stretch her neck to look up at Lisa.

'Yes?'

'I've come to visit Sarah.'

'Well, you've rung the wrong bell,' and she made to push the door shut. Sarah appeared round the curve of the stairs. 'Don't take any notice of her,' she called. 'Miserable old cow. This is a friend of mine,' she yelled into the woman's ear and, beckoning for Lisa to follow, she raced back upstairs, taking the steps two at a time, falling every now and then and giggling, until she reached the top.

Sarah had two rooms, a sitting-room and a bedroom, with a tiny kitchen on the landing below and a bathroom tucked into the roof.

'It's great.' Lisa sank down on to a sofa.

'It's all right,' Sarah said carelessly, knocking over an ashtray. 'Smoke?' She waved a packet of Rizla papers at her.

Lisa wavered for a moment, her ears ringing out a warning. 'All right.'

Sarah and Lisa sat on the floor and passed a bulging joint of black Moroccan back and forth between them.

'How's Ruby?' Sarah asked.

Lisa, careful not to give too much away and fighting with the first flush of fear as she inhaled, answered, 'Fine. How's Tom?'

Sarah blew a succession of flawed smoke rings into the air. 'Haven't you heard?'

'No.'

She blinked slowly and Lisa, unable to restrain herself, asked, 'Haven't I heard what?'

'We've fallen out. Tom and me. We're not talking.'

Lisa couldn't imagine what would turn Sarah against her brother. What she wouldn't put up with to be on his side. Lisa thought of the time Tom had rolled a joint, especially for Sarah and herself, and watched them as they smoked it. He had encouraged them when they got the giggles, when they raided the larder and fell over on the lawn, only to tell them afterwards that the joint they'd smoked was packed with oregano, Old Holborn and two dried leaves. That might have been the time to turn against Tom, but they hadn't even discussed it. They had kept their embarrassment to themselves and learnt their own private lesson.

'He stopped me from seeing Philip,' Sarah said.

Philip was the man in the photo. The handsome man Marguerite had admired on the bus.

Lisa was amazed. 'How?'

'How what?'

'How did he stop you seeing Philip?' She wondered if Sarah had heard of feminism, but didn't ask in case it was something she had long since given up on.

'He turned me against him,' Sarah said. 'He referred to him as "the Chin" and called him a sleaze-ball . . . He gagged on his aftershave and mimicked his voice on the phone, until I, I just sort of went off him.'

'Christ.'

Sarah was rolling another joint. She stopped and looked at Lisa with her eyes screwed up. 'But you must *really* hate Tom.'

'Me?' Lisa flinched. 'Not really.'

'You should.' Sarah struck a match.

Lisa didn't ask why. She didn't want to hear anything she hadn't already guessed at. She held the smoke so long in her lungs it evaporated and she had to lie down on the floor. Microscopic animals were crawling over her eyes and her tongue was thick and white in her mouth. Never again, she promised herself, never again, she vowed, as she continued obediently to inhale. Sarah lay down next to her. She told her about Philip and how in love they had been. How he had bought her a dozen champagne roses and taken her out to dinner on her birthday. How he had kissed her ankles and said they were exquisite. Philip had travelled, and nothing in the whole wide world, he said, was as beautiful as one of Sarah's ankles.

'Couldn't you get back together?' Lisa asked dreamily.

But apparently Philip had been driven into the arms of Sarah's cousin Tanya, and now she had to listen to daily reports of their happiness from various members of her family who still maintained he was a prig.

Lisa started to laugh. She couldn't help herself. The animals had stopped crawling and her heart was as calm and sluggish as a river. She choked and spluttered and cried with laughter until she had to roll on to her stomach to bury her face in the carpet.

'Lisa.' Sarah tugged at her. 'Lisa, come to the shop with me. I need some ice cream.'

Lisa sat up, suddenly starving. 'Cake.'

They bought Arctic Roll, a yellow sponge with an ice-cream centre, and hurried back to the flat. Sarah ran a hot bath. 'So we won't freeze while we're eating it,' she said, and they were so overcome with a fit of laughter they had to crawl up to the bathroom on their hands and knees. They sat in the bath with dinner plates of Arctic Roll and discussed possible plans for revenge.

Sarah was eager to involve Ruby. 'Where's Ruby living?' she asked. And Lisa, her mouth full of ice-cold sponge, shook her head.

'You don't know? Really?'

'Really.'

Sarah believed her. She wasn't supposed to, but she did. The bath water was cooling and the arctic centre of the cake had begun to melt. There was only one towel and Sarah got out first. Lisa had fallen in her estimation. She could feel herself falling. She lay back in the luke-warm water. 'I could try and find out.'

'Hmm.' Sarah was unconvinced.

Lisa slid down between the taps and let her head sink below the surface of the water. She held her breath and thought how she and Ruby had played this game as children. Counting out each other's stamina in bananas, one banana, two banana, practising for the dream of deep-sea diving. They hadn't heard of oxygen masks or snorkels then. Lisa burst back up. 'Ten banana,' she said.

Sarah handed her the wet towel.

Lisa had always been good at keeping secrets. She was so good at it that no one even suspected she had any to keep. She had often found herself having to listen to something she had been holding sacred and to herself for years. Sometimes the secret she had been entrusted with transpired not really to be a secret at all. It was some-thing openly discussed, only in a particular tone of voice. Lisa wondered now if Ruby's Belgravia address was one of those secrets. For all she knew, Sarah was the only person in London who didn't know it. For all she knew, Tom and Jimmy Bright were regular visitors and Mar-lene's boyfriend had long since been pacified. Lisa shiv-ered and forced herself out of the tepid water. She didn't know why she was bothering to tangle her thoughts up like this when even if she wanted to tell she couldn't. Her throat clammed up like the narrowest neck of a bottle and the words stayed wrapped around her ribs.

'Lisa!' Sarah shouted. 'What are you doing up there?' And Lisa, still dripping, hurried down to join her.

The effects of the black Moroccan had worn off and Sarah was in a sulk. She sat by the gas fire drying her hair and brooding. Lisa made a desperate attempt to win her back. 'I was thinking of having a party.'

Sarah looked up.

'We could invite Tom and work in some revenge.'

Sarah swept the hair back from her face. Her eyes lit up. 'Like what?'

'Like . . . I'm not sure, but we could work something out.'

'Invite Ruby for one thing.'

'Yes.' Lisa wasn't sure.

They planned the party for New Year's Eve. They drew up a list of people.

'I'd have it here,' Sarah said, 'if it wasn't for that old hag downstairs.'

'It's all right,' Lisa assured her. 'My mother will be away then, anyway.'

Ruby hadn't spent a Christmas with her family since leaving home. This year they were going to some friends of Marguerite's in Norfolk, and Lisa begged Ruby to come. Ruby lay stretched out on the sofa with the television turned down low. She said her whole body ached. She said she thought she had flu. She said she might come, maybe, but that Tom had invited her to spend Christmas with his family in Wales.

'I thought you didn't see Tom any more.'

Ruby shifted uncomfortably on the sofa. 'Shhh.'

Marlene was walking through on her way from the bathroom to the kitchen, her hair bound up in a towel, and looking like an Ethiopian princess. When she was safely out of earshot, Ruby whispered, 'I see him sometimes, when I can get out.' She sighed. 'Marlene says she gave up everything and now the least I can do is give up Tom.'

Lisa didn't know what to say, so she told her about Tom's campaign against Philip. She told the story as brutally as she could, with all sympathy reserved for Sarah. Ruby just laughed. When she laughed, it made her stomach ache and so she stopped.

'Why don't you come to Wales too?' She squeezed Lisa's hand. 'I wish you would.'

Ruby had given up her East End accent since moving into Belgravia. The longer she was there the more like her neighbours she sounded. She had even started to have her laundry collected and delivered by a private service that starched and folded every item. 'Oh do come,' she said. 'It would be *such* fun if you did.'

'I don't think so.' Lisa pulled her hand away. She wanted to add that she hadn't been invited.

Marlene, still in her towelling turban, reappeared with a bowl of cornflakes and a phial of pink nail polish.

'Lisa wondered if you'd make her up,' Ruby said to cover any talk of Christmas, and Marlene, smiling and setting aside her cereal, began to work an elaborate magic over Lisa's pale face with an assortment of smudgy pastel brushes.

Lisa called Janey to invite her to the party. Janey was so excited she whooped down the phone. She had already promised to babysit her sister's little boy, but she intended to get out of it if it was the last thing she did.

Lisa phoned Sarah regularly to discuss how many packets of Twiglets and Hula Hoops to buy, and how much drink. Neither of them mentioned Christmas. 'Won't there be something special in Wales for New Year?' she asked, worried that Sarah might not be back in time for the party. But Sarah said, 'Not at all. It's the same dirge the world over.' She was still depressed over Philip.

Sarah had considered inviting Philip, in the hope of luring him away from her cousin, but she was stopped short in her plan by the news that he was taking Tanya to Paris and wouldn't be back until the third of January. 'Well, New Year may not be quite the same dirge in Paris,' she added with a dry laugh.

Lisa was relying on her father to give her some money.

Lisa's father didn't celebrate Christmas and wasn't the kind of person to go shopping for presents, but she was certain that as long as she saw him at some point before she went away to Norfolk he would be bound to offer her something.

She called Ruby. Ruby was engaged. Lisa spent so much time in the payphones on the Old Street roundabout that the newsagents where she went for change all knew her. She had a purse full of two-pence pieces that weighed down the pocket of her coat. She redialled Ruby's number.

'Hello?' Ruby's voice was thin and far away.

'Hello, Ruby?'

'Oh Lisa, it's you, could you ring back, I'm waiting for an important call. Do you mind?'

'No, no, of course not,' Lisa said. 'I'll ring back in five minutes.' And her fingers slipped over themselves in her haste to replace the receiver.

It took Lisa another half an hour to get through. When Ruby finally answered, her voice was so faint she could hardly hear her.

'Ruby, are you all right?'

'What? Oh you know, it's just . . .' It was as if she didn't have the strength to go on talking.

'Is Marlene there?' Lisa asked.

'She's gone out.'

It was only eight o'clock. Marlene never went anywhere before midnight.

'Are you sure everything's all right?'

She could hear Ruby hesitating. 'What?' she said eventually.

Lisa wanted to get at her and shake her. 'I'm coming over,' and when Ruby didn't answer, she hung up.

*

Lisa caught the train to Hyde Park Corner, paid one stop from Green Park, and ran all the way to the narrow street behind the German embassy. She rang the bell, keeping her finger pressed down shrilly, and when no one answered, she remembered, and rang her code of three short rings. 'Ruby!' she shouted through the letter-box. 'Ruby!!'

Marlene's soft voice made her jump on the other side of the door. 'Lisa, is that you?'

Ruby sat on the sofa, bright-eyed and revitalized. 'Hi, Lisa,' she said as if she were surprised to see her, and Lisa, confused and unable to explain the dead weight of panic in her throat, made out she was just passing and could only stay five minutes.

When Lisa changed trains at King's Cross, she walked on to an escalator going the wrong way and was thrown off by the force of its moving steps. As her foot touched down, the step came up and hit her in the soles of the feet so that she lost balance and was thrown to the floor. She couldn't get up. She sat in a huddle in the rush of people and fought the long, angry tears that slipped from her eyes. There had been something personal in the way that iron step had thrown her off. She couldn't get it out of her mind. The coats and bags of a swarm of people brushed over her shoulders. They streamed around her like a line of marching ants, eager not to miss their train. She looked up, and through her tears she caught a woman hesitating, wavering with her conscience, wondering if she should help. Lisa glared. She defied her to approach, and, when the woman backed away and stepped guiltily on to her escalator, Lisa despised her lack of courage and watched her scornfully as she disappeared underground, bodily bit by bit.

Lisa stood up and dusted down her coat. Her hands were shaking and she felt the blood rushing around her head, pumping hot and cold inside her ears. It occurred to her she might be ill. She might have Ruby's flu. Or a late reaction to Max's last month's mumps. This thought consoled her and gave her the strength to descend the three flights of escalator to the Northern Line.

Lisa found her mother at Heidi's, drinking cider with Steen. Max was asleep under a coat.

'Actually, I'm not feeling well,' she said when Steen pressed a glass on her. Marguerite offered to take her back and make her a hot drink.

Steen wouldn't hear of it. 'I make the best hot toddy this side of the border,' and he disappeared into the kitchen.

Lisa cradled the cup in her hands and waited for the drink to cool. She could smell the whisky rising when she blew on it, and with the first sip the bitter taste of lemon stung the inside of her nose. 'It's good,' she said, as all eyes rested on her. It wasn't until something almost unnoticed slipped down her throat that it occurred to her Steen might have added an extra ingredient. 'It's good,' she said again, stretching her eyes with innocence to add, 'What did you put in it?'

'Ah-ha,' Steen winked, and in an exaggerated Scottish accent, 'I'll no be telling my secret recipe.' He laughed quite openly around the room.

Lisa froze. The insides of her stomach turned to water and she set down her drink, hurriedly picking it up again, before rushing to the toilet. She set the cup on the floor where she could see it. She kept her eye on it, hardly daring to blink. She sat on the toilet with her head in her hands. All she could think of was her mother saying, 'I remember when I used to drop acid, it made me want to have a good shit.' Lisa knew her mother wasn't lying when she talked about her youth. She talked about drugs as happily and easily as if it were a walk in the park. She even had a photo of herself on an acid trip, she and Ruby, toddlers, crayoning at the very edge, and Marguerite leaning back on one elbow with stars in her eyes and unearthly strands of white matter swirling around her head.

Lisa joined the others in the sitting-room, her mug, still warm, held against her chest. She sat against a wall, slowly sipping in an attempt to appear normal.

Marguerite came and sat next to her. 'Are you feeling any better?'

Lisa nodded, and then she did something unforgivable, she passed her mother the poisoned cup. 'Have a sip,' she offered, 'it's good.'

Lisa closed her eyes. Every inch of skin on her body was stretched with waiting and she had no way of knowing whether what part of twenty minutes was up or not. Her mother took a gulp and handed back the cup. 'You're letting it get cold,' she scolded.

Lisa watched her mother with terrible sidelong glances. She had lost track of herself and the seething fear dissolved all reason in her brain. She was holding on with her finger nails. Scratching at gravel. Her heartbeats cut into her like flint.

'Shall we go?' Marguerite called to her through thin ice and, with Max still sleeping and wrapped in his coat, they descended Heidi's staircase and climbed their own to their flat on the first floor.

There must have been music playing at Steen's and

Heidi's because as soon as they opened the door Lisa's ears filled up with silence. Marguerite put Max to bed and ran herself a bath. Lisa watched her closely for suspicious signs of the hot toddy having taken effect. She followed her around the tiny flat and sat on the edge of her bath while she lay, languid, in the water. 'Are you all right?' she asked, trying to remember if she had ever known her mother before to bathe at midnight. Marguerite squinted at her. The air between them hummed with cold electric waves. 'Are *you* all right?' She turned her head, and Lisa nodded in earnest that she was.

Lisa offered to wash her mother's back so that she could peer round her shoulder to get a glimpse of the secret state of her thoughts. She needed to see into her eyes. Once or twice she caught Marguerite glancing strangely back at her, and she had a thousand explanations for these looks. She could feel the strands of her thoughts twisting round themselves like the steel spokes of a wheel.

Lisa continued to sit on the edge of the bath while her mother stepped dripping from the water, dried herself and pulled a clean, white nightdress over her head. 'Goodnight,' she said, and she closed the door to her and Max's narrow room.

Lisa crawled between the sheets of her own bed and lay awake until the dull shades of the dawn breaking over Peerless Street convinced her she was spared, and she fell into a thankful and exhausted sleep.

The day before they were due to go away for Christmas, Marguerite received a letter from a doctor in Harley Street. Lisa watched the colour drain from her mother's face as she read it over breakfast.

Ruby was going in for 'the Cure'. She had been admitted to a drug rehabilitation centre in Ealing.

'But Ruby doesn't have a problem with drugs,' Marguerite gasped, 'they must be mad!'

Lisa continued to spread Marmite thinly over buttered toast. She cut soldiers for Max to dip into his egg.

'Why does no one tell me anything?' Tears of rage sprang from Marguerite's eyes like hard, glass beads. 'I mean all young people experiment, it's normal, there's nothing wrong in it. Is there?'

Lisa shrugged.

Marguerite put her hands up to her face. 'Why will no one tell me what's going on?' she sobbed.

Ruby was allowed no contact with the outside world until after Christmas. The hospital gave permission to visit on the Saturday before New Year. Lisa wondered if a similar letter had been sent to her father. She wrote him a last-minute Christmas card with the vague intention of alerting him to the facts. *Dear Dad, Happy Christmas.* She couldn't think what else to write. After about an hour of doodling she added, *Love from Lisa.* She ran with it to the post office, where she bought a stamp and posted it before she could change her mind. She was under the impression she had written much more than she had.

She called Sarah from the payphone to warn her the party might have to be cancelled. There was no answer. Lisa wondered who else she should call. She flicked through her address book and realized, a little sadly but with some relief, that the only person she had actually invited was Janey. She was about to call her when she saw Marguerite appear from the sloping mouth of the short cut and head towards the row of phone boxes. She swung open the door of the booth.

'I thought I might find you here.' Marguerite squeezed in beside her. 'I've been thinking, I don't know if we should go to Norfolk.'

'Why not?'

'I just feel so terrible going off with Ruby stuck in that place.'

Lisa knew what she meant. 'But it's not as if we can do anything.' Ruby was not even allowed to receive a card. It was a rule of the hospital, to avoid causing undue distress to those without friends or relations.

Marguerite sighed. She rested her ten pence in its slot and dialled. 'Babs?' The money clattered home.

Lisa slid down the wall of the booth and waited for her to finish. Babs didn't sound as if she was too worried about whether they came for Christmas or not. 'Whatever,' Lisa heard her say. She was an old friend of Marguerite's from the sixties. Someone she had met when she worked as a nude model at the Slade.

'Did you used to model when you were pregnant with me?' Lisa asked as they walked the long way home. Marguerite had left the subject of Christmas open. 'We'll either be there or we won't.'

'What?' She looked at Lisa. 'With Ruby I did, but you . . . Oh I can't remember.' Marguerite had once said that when she was pregnant with Ruby she lived on oysters and champagne, but that throughout her second pregnancy she had survived on a diet of baked beans and porridge. Lisa was never sure what was intended by this particular anecdote, but it made her blanch with guilt when she thought of it.

Lisa and Marguerite drove to Ealing in the butcher's van. Max was to spend the day with Frances and little Brendan, well stocked with paper and crayons and without his cap gun. He had to be physically prised out of his armour.

Marguerite rarely used the van now they lived in London. Whenever she did, it either broke down or she became hopelessly lost and unable to trace her way back to the Old Street roundabout. Lisa promised to map-read. She chose a route through the centre of the city, which was a mistake, and then they got caught up in the traffic heading south out of London. They were low on petrol and the engine had begun to overheat. Marguerite swore and accelerated furiously. 'The first person who offers me fifty quid for this wreck can drive it away.'

'Oh Mum,' Lisa moaned as they sped past the hospital turn-off for the second time.

'The Cure' was in a wing of Hanworth Hospital. Hanworth Hospital was a mental hospital and was the kind of place Lisa envisaged in her very darkest moments ending up. It was a large, gloomy, Victorian building in the middle of a field. Lisa took her mother's hand as they walked down a pale green, windowless corridor. The air was thick with the drifting smell of cabbage. They pushed their way through spongy rubber doors, hoping to find an orderly, a nurse, or even a patient, but each green corridor led on to another and another, with never any sign of anyone at all. Eventually they found a staircase and climbed out of what they now realized was the basement. Lisa knew she shouldn't, but she couldn't resist letting her gaze slide sideways, left and right, through the open doors of desperate, lemon-yellow wards. Twisted old men, gnarled up like trees, stood staring into space, or lay like small, ill children on their beds. They traipsed down endless corridors, past whole wards of silence, and then a shout would break out and a struggle and the sounds of hearts pounding and black shoes slipping on the lino.

Lisa's terror ran up and down her arm and trembled in her mother's hand. They walked so close they almost tripped each other up. Eventually they caught sight of a doctor, his white coat flapping as he sped towards them, his body swaying from side to side to keep up with his legs, like a school boy who knows he mustn't run.

'Doctor.' Marguerite tried to flag him down. 'Excuse me.' The doctor, without interrupting his pace, twisted, looked at his watch, shook it at them and, with a mumbled apology, billowed by.

Lisa and Marguerite walked on. There were nurses behind the walls of the wards. Nurses who would be happy to give them directions. They kept to the corridor, defying each other to mention it.

Lisa had a present for Ruby. It was a bracelet of mother-of-pearl that she had bought in the market at Camden Lock. It was the most beautiful thing she had ever seen and she had to wrench away all thoughts of keeping it or even wearing it for one day and wrap it immediately in tissue-paper. It fastened with a silver clasp. Marguerite had a pot of blue hyacinths and a bottle of concentrated apple juice.

Eventually they came out at a stairwell with a large stained-glass window and a signpost to the chapel. A man sat at a desk by double wooden doors. 'We're looking for the Drug Rehabilitation Unit,' Marguerite said, and he looked up and smiled. 'Oh you mean the Cure.' They had to go out through the double doors, along a path and round to the back of the building. They were to follow the signs to Ward 2E.

Ruby was in a bed at the very end of the ward. Lisa recognized her short spiky hair on the pillow even though her face was turned away from them.

'Hello, darling,' Marguerite said, bending down to kiss her.

'Mum!' Ruby struggled to sit up with a glint of real enthusiasm. 'Am I glad to see you.'

Lisa squeezed between them and kissed Ruby on the cheek. Ruby was papery thin and her shoulder was made from the bones of a little bird. 'Happy Christmas,' she said, and she thrust her present on to Ruby's lap. She had been holding it so tightly the wrapping had gone soggy.

'Happy Christmas.' Marguerite moved round to the other side and sat down on the edge of her bed.

'Ow!' Ruby scowled in pain, and pulled her foot away. 'Can't you get a chair to sit on?'

Marguerite leapt up without losing her cheerful expression and looked round wildly for a chair. There were none to be seen.

'Aren't you going to open your presents?' Lisa said in an attempt to regain the moment.

'Yes, open your presents,' Marguerite agreed and she scooped the hyacinth out of its plastic bag. Its blue flower had somehow snapped during the journey and hung now by a strand of thick green stalk. Marguerite didn't seem to notice. She placed it tenderly on the bedside table while Lisa hovered anxiously for Ruby to unwrap her present. 'I hope you like it,' she encouraged, almost unable to endure the suspense. Ruby picked at the Sellotape with unenthusiastic fingers. Lisa had wrapped the bracelet in three layers of different-coloured tissue. She could sense her sister's irritation as she peeled away the paper. Eventually a white glint of pearl showed through and Ruby pulled out the bracelet.

'Oh, I brought you some apple juice,' Marguerite said at the exact moment that Ruby set eyes on the bracelet. 'You just have to mix it with water.'

Ruby put the bracelet to one side and took the heavy bottle.

'Thanks.' She let her arm rest with it alongside her body. 'Thanks.' She kept her fingers tightly round the bottleneck and closed her eyes as if she had been overtaken by exhaustion. Lisa and Marguerite stared down at her. 'I'll go and find some chairs,' Marguerite said, and she tiptoed away. Lisa sat very carefully on the edge of the bed and waited for Ruby to open her eyes. Ruby had the most perfect eyelids. They were shaped like shells with arched eyebrows above and a spray of smart, bright lashes below. Lisa had once taken a photo-booth photograph of herself in their local Woolworth's in an attempt to discover whether or not this particular feature of Ruby's had been duplicated in herself, but the photo had shown a pair of wide, heavy lids, deep-set and shadowy under brows without a hint of an arch.

Marguerite returned with two chairs. They sat side by side at the top of Ruby's bed and waited for her to wake up. After half an hour they decided it was best to leave.

Lisa gave a last glance at the mother-of-pearl bracelet nestling in its bed of tissue and considered taking it back. Ruby might not even notice. She hadn't even looked at it. She hadn't even tried it on. She looked down at the arrogant arches of Ruby's eyebrows and felt a wave of bitter rage against her lack of gratitude.

Lisa had high hopes for her first New Year in London. She rang Sarah in Wales to tell her about the cancelled party and to ask if she wanted to make an alternative plan, but her money ran out before anything final was agreed upon, and by the time she'd managed to rustle up another tenpence it seemed everyone had gone out or had moved into a part of the house where it was impossible to hear the telephone.

Janey had suggested they have the party anyway. 'Can't your Mum just go into another room?' And Lisa tried to explain to her about Peerless Flats and the bedroom and how there was barely enough space for the bunks.

Up until the very last moment Lisa believed that something fantastic was bound to happen. She, Marguerite and Max spent the whole day playing dominoes and waiting for the rain to stop, and when they eventually had to accept it might fall for ever in sharp grey splinters against their only real window they decided to go out and buy provisions. Lisa stuck a note to the door which said 'Back soon' in case someone were to call while they were out.

The rain was so fierce that halfway to the bus stop they sheltered in a doorway and discussed whether it mightn't be wiser to turn back. 'What about my sponge fingers?' Max demanded from under his carrier-bag hat, and they decided to persevere. There was a supermarket at the Angel where Marguerite said they could buy a treat each as it was New Year's Eve and the last day of the 1970s. Lisa took Max's hand and they wandered up and down the aisles looking for sponge fingers. They found them under 'cake ingredients', and then Max changed his mind and decided he wanted a half-pound packet of marzipan. They found Marguerite by the fruit and vegetables, considering a mound of fresh spinach. 'Oh Mum,' they both whined, and Lisa suggested she get something a little more compatible with marzipan and twenty John Player Special, which was what she had chosen for herself. Marguerite eventually decided on a bottle of cider and a packet of white chocolate buttons.

It was raining so hard when they arrived back at Peerless Street that they could see the drops like bullets bouncing in the road. They jumped over the puddles in the open entrance of the building and raced up to their flat. Marguerite put down the plastic bag of food and rummaged in her pockets. Then she rummaged again, more slowly. 'You haven't got the key, have you?' She looked at Lisa with a defeated face, and Lisa shook her head.

Max kicked the door. 'Let me in!' he yelled, leaving a little wet footprint on the wood. He put his eye to the keyhole. 'Mr Fox,' he called in a persuasive voice, 'can we come in now? I've got some nice things for supper.' Lisa pushed him to one side and tried to pick the lock with a hairgrip she found in her purse. Marguerite had given up. She sat on the top step and opened the chocolate buttons. 'Don't eat them all,' Lisa said and she and Max went and sat next to her to make sure. Once they'd finished the chocolate they opened the cider and Max allowed them each one tiny bite of his marzipan. Lisa scratched her cigarette lottery ticket with a coin and for a single spiralling moment she thought that she'd won. 'Close, very close.' Marguerite consoled her. She'd simply misread the numbers.

Lisa's coat was not waterproof and now the damp of the wool was starting to seep through into her bones. 'We can't stay here all night,' she said.

Max moved closer to her and shivered. 'Why not?' he begged through chattering teeth. 'I'll make a tent and we can sleep in a hammock made out of rats' tails and I'll stand at the entrance to the cave and say, "Who goes there?"'

'Shhh.' Lisa thought she heard a voice echoing up from the stairwell.

'Who goes there?' Max jumped up, brandishing his imaginary sword.

Tom's bedraggled head and shoulders appeared round the twist in the stairs, followed closely by Sarah in a waterproof hat.

'We're having a picnic.' Marguerite shook the cider bottle at them. 'Why don't you join us?'

Tom and Sarah ambled up the stairs. 'Happy New Year,' they said politely and they all exchanged kisses. Max offered Tom a bite of his marzipan, keeping his thumb close to the edge so that he wouldn't take too much. He then commenced to whisper a secret list of all his weapons into Tom's ear. Marguerite asked Sarah about her job in the clothes shop and told her about her own unsuccessful attempts at employment. Lisa took a long swig from the cider bottle and wondered when it would occur to Tom and Sarah that her family were not spending New Year's Eve on the landing on a purely eccentric whim but because they had in fact locked themselves out.

Half an hour later when Sarah asked if she could use the bathroom the truth was discovered.

'It's all right,' Tom said, standing back and breathing through his nose, 'I'll get you in,' and he took a running kick at the door and burst it open with his foot, shattering the lock and cracking away part of the frame.

Max ran into the room with his arms outstretched and spun around like a bat. 'You're brilliant, you're brilliant, will you be my friend?' he screamed.

Tom was so exhausted he had to lie down on the floor. 'Do you think he's going to be all right?' Lisa asked as she tried to hold Max back from using his outstretched body as a trampoline. Marguerite brought him a cup of cider to revive him and Lisa lit him a cigarette and held it to his mouth. His face had gone a deathly tallow-white and his lips were bloodless. There was a part of Lisa that worried he might have stopped breathing and she allowed herself to look into his face with an open reserve of love. Tom recovered and caught her. He smiled slyly and grabbed her wrist as she pulled away. He pulled her down and tried to kiss her. The others had all moved through to the bedroom to inspect Max's collection of fishing flies. 'Do you know where you can find good worms round here?' she heard him asking Sarah.

Lisa knelt over Tom as he smoked. 'Do you care about me?' he asked, his eyes narrow, and Lisa, unable to decide whether or not this was a trick that would be stored and later used against her, didn't answer.

Tom and Sarah were going on to a party they had heard about in a disused fire station in Battersea. They asked Lisa if she wanted to go, but even though she longed to, she felt unable to leave her mother alone in a flat where the door no longer locked or even closed, but

139

hung shakily from one hinge. 'If you want to go, you must,' Marguerite insisted, but behind her smile little flecks of fear swam in her eyes.

Lisa saw Tom and Sarah down to the street. It was still raining but the hail had turned to a fine grey drizzle. Tom kissed her distractedly on the cheek. 'I nearly forgot,' he said. 'Where the fuck has Ruby got to?'

Lisa shuffled her feet and pulled her cardigan up over her head. 'What's that?' she said, as if his voice hadn't carried through the mist of the rain.

'Oh come on, Tom.' Sarah pulled her hat around her ears, 'I'm getting soaked.'

'I've got to find Ruby,' Tom shouted, and Lisa, thinking she might burst into tears, ran back into the arched entrance of Peerless Flats.

Frances had given up on the council to find her anywhere permanent to live and gone back to her family in Ireland. A single man with paralysis in his left leg moved into her old flat, which, apart from being a scandal as it was on the fourth floor, meant that when Lisa and Marguerite next visited Ruby at Hanworth Hospital, they had to take Max with them.

Ruby was out of bed and dressed uncharacteristically in a Laura Ashley smock with a frill around the bottom. She seemed quite cheerful and took them for tea in the canteen. The canteen was a white wooden building separate from the hospital. They had to walk down a path through the park to get to it. Ruby giggled and told them to watch out for a woman in a red ribbed nylon jumper.

The woman was a few feet ahead of them in the queue and they watched her shuffle forward to order her tea. It was poured for her in a green cup on a saucer, which she clutched with both hands as she inched her way over to the nearest table. Her arms shook so violently as she walked that the tea splashed out in great milky spurts and left a watery trail over the lino. The woman didn't seem to notice but moved on with her eyes wide and fixed on her destination, so that it was only when she arrived that she discovered with a look of vague bewilderment that her cup was empty. Ruby tittered and nudged Lisa in the ribs as the trembling woman promptly rejoined the queue.

Max was very quiet. He stayed close to Marguerite and didn't ask for anything from the counter display of two-fingered Kit-Kats and miniature packets of short-bread. They took their three teas and a glass of flat lemonade and sat at a table by the window. Lisa sipped her tea and watched her mother's reflection in the glass, summoning up the right words to say to Ruby.

'You're looking much better,' she managed eventually, and Ruby smiled and then waved at a woman who was staring over at them and mouthing elaborately, 'Is that your family?' Ruby mouthed back, 'Yes,' and the woman sat down at a table, alone with a mound of biscuits, and began to eat.

'Who's that?' Marguerite asked, and Ruby lowered her voice. 'Christine. She's in the next bed to me.'

Lisa wanted to ask what Christine was doing in Hanworth Hospital. She was middle-aged and heavily made up, with bright blue eyeshadow and a smear of rock-pink lipstick. She looked too old to be a drug addict.

'Why's she in here?' Marguerite asked instead, and Ruby leaned across the table and whispered dramati-cally, 'She's an alcoholic!'

When Ruby's friend had eaten all her biscuits, she came over to their table. 'Hello, I'm Ruby's friend, nice to see you.' She smiled a big smile that crinkled the end of her nose.

'This is me Mum,' Ruby said, picking up the loop and whine of her south London accent, 'and this is me sister, Lisa.'

'And me,' Max said.

'And this is Christine,' Ruby continued.

'Hello, yes, I'm Christine,' Christine said, and she leant

over to Marguerite and said confidentially, 'Oh, you've got a lovely daughter, you really have. What a lovely girl.'

Marguerite blushed and nodded and eventually Christine left them to rejoin the queue.

Ruby was only allowed to be away from her ward for forty minutes at a time, so they left the canteen and walked back through the park. Ruby put her arm through Lisa's and told her about Christine: how Christine was married to a crook who insisted to this day he earned an honest living as a plumber. Christine's husband wouldn't allow her to leave the house or talk to anyone except for him, and so she began to drink until she was drinking so heavily that she needed three bottles of vodka just to see her through the day. Christine thought everything might have been all right if a doctor hadn't prescribed Mandrax to cheer her up and if she hadn't been overcome by the desire to paint the blue carpet in the front room red. 'There's only one thing in her life she's really proud of,' Ruby said.

Lisa couldn't guess what it was.

'She never let her husband see her without makeup. Not in nine years of married life!'

When they arrived back at Ward 2E there was a man sitting on Ruby's bed writing a note.

'Dad!' Ruby ran over to greet him. She almost tripped over a crate of fresh fruit wrapped around with ribbon that was resting up against her bedside table.

'Hello, Dad,' Lisa said and he smiled past her and nervously up at Marguerite. There was an uncomfortable silence and then Max, who had been studying the oranges and lychees and winter raspberries clustered round the centrepiece of pineapple in the giant crate, began in a sudden frenzy to tear open the shiny plastic wrapping.

All three women rushed to his side. Even a passing nurse stopped to comment on the unruliness of his behaviour. 'Max, Max, Max,' they scolded, and then Marguerite added, 'I think it's time we were off.'

Marguerite did a U-turn in the car park and roared out through the hospital gates without bothering to change gear. Lisa had wanted to stay, peeling lychees and gossiping with Ruby, while they lounged with their father in the day-room. She hadn't even had a chance to ask him if he'd received her Christmas card.

'Give us a bit,' she snapped at Max who was sitting in the back of the van, eating a tangerine he had spirited out in the sleeve of his jumper. 'NO,' Max yelled, stuffing the whole remains into his mouth, and he lay down backwards in the spare tyre, and kicked his arms and legs as if it were a rubber ring.

'Brat!' And for a moment Lisa thought of opening the car door and hurling herself out on to the road.

Lisa started back at college for the spring term. The Full Time Speech and Drama course had moved its focus from Stanislavsky to Brecht, which meant that, whereas last term the students were encouraged to believe absolutely in everything they did and said, now, when acting, they were asked to remember that they were in a play, and that they had a duty to the audience to remind them of this fact. There were techniques that could be used, winking, or talking in asides, or even giving information on the plot straight out into the front row without any pretence at mystery or disguise. Lisa felt completely thrown. For her the whole point of acting was the licence it gave you to become another person, protected by a stage set and someone else's words, and now Denise the method teacher, whose main criticism had always been 'I don't believe it!', began interrupting the action of a scene to ask what the actors thought was going on in terms of the play's integral message.

'What type of actress are you going to be, Brechtian or Stanislavskian?' Janey asked Lisa in the canteen.

Lisa wasn't sure. Really she just wanted to be Julie Christie in *Doctor Zhivago* and wear a fur hat and a tailored coat with buttons down the front. She mentioned this to Janey. Janey rolled her eyes and sniggered, and then told her quite seriously she'd never get into proper drama school if she admitted to those sorts of ambitions. 'It's not fashionable to want to be a film star.'

Lisa made a note of this under Denise's list of books to read:

> *The Good Woman of Setzuan*, Brecht
> *Mother Courage*, Brecht
> and *The Theatre of Revolt*

Lisa had also added *Where the Wild Things Are*, a book about a boy called Max, which she thought she might be able to get from the children's section of the library.

Steen had come round on New Year's Day to fix the broken door. 'Burglars?'

'No, no, just a friend,' Marguerite assured him.

Steen said that really the whole frame of the door needed replacing, but he would try and patch it together for the time being.

Lisa could hardly bear to be in the same room as Steen. The moment she saw him, an electric ringing started up in her ears. She and her mother had never discussed the hot toddy and the strange looks they had exchanged in the bathroom, but since that night Lisa had been almost unable to eat or drink anything that she had not supervised herself, and if for any reason she was distracted from a meal, she preferred to abandon it rather than take the risk that it might have become contaminated in the moment she was forced to look away. Lisa became so thin that her periods stopped, and when she lay in bed at night she could feel her heart beating in her ear. There were days at college when it took all her energy to fight through the crackling and freezing of the inside of her head and to keep the twitching of her eye to a minimum. Sometimes when she turned her head the bones in her neck cracked so loudly that she was surprised the whole class didn't rush over to see whether it was broken, but no one ever mentioned it, and Lisa was so grateful for this that she found herself praying silently at night that she might have the strength to keep up the façade.

Steen mended the door so that it closed and locked, but there was something irrevocably damaged about the catch, which meant it could be opened with a gentle shove of the shoulder, and even though Marguerite reported it to the caretaker, and even demanded several times that it be replaced, nothing was ever done and in a short time, as they continued to mislay their keys, Lisa and Marguerite both found themselves increasingly reliant on the flimsiness of the lock.

It was half-term and Marguerite decided to go back to the country for a long weekend. Lisa, although she had some days off college, couldn't bring herself to visit the village where she had grown up, knowing how incapable she would be of matching the impact made by Ruby on her triumphant return two years before. She decided to stay in London.

That first night Lisa luxuriated in the emptiness of the flat, relieved to be alone for once with the ringing and twitching she held inside her like a leper. She prepared herself a meal. Rice, and vegetables cooked with a bay leaf and soya sauce, exactly to her mother's own recipe. She moved around the kitchen, humming along to the limited and now familiar collection of Leonard Cohen records played by the man in the flat above.

Lisa laid a place for herself at the table and set down the heaped plate of food, with a small salad in a bowl beside it, and a glass of water at its head. She was about to sit down when she realized how desperately she needed to pee. She leapt up to dash to the toilet before her food had time to cool, but as she moved away her eye was caught by the vulnerable leaves of her salad and the multicoloured vegetables that camouflaged the grains of rice, and, without allowing herself to contemplate the implications of her behaviour, she loaded the dishes on to a tray and carried it through to the toilet, where she positioned it in the doorway in such a way she could

148

keep her eye on it at all times. She had to reach out for the taps to wash her hands and search blindly about for a towel. Eventually Lisa arrived back at the table, where she unloaded her supper. She had to pretend her mother was sitting opposite before she could summon the strength to lift her fork. The saliva in her mouth had curdled white and bitter, giving the fat grains of rice a metallic taste as she chewed them dully together between her teeth.

Lisa put her unfinished meal in the fridge and went through to the sitting-room to watch television. The television was tiny, and black and white and had been a present from Frances, who said it was too heavy and awkward to carry back to Ireland. Lisa lay on her bed and turned the dial between each of the three channels. There was nothing on that she wanted to watch but she left it tuned to a modern ballet, in which minuscule black figures flickered about on a background of grey. Lisa's bed, which also served as a sofa, was set against the wall next to the window, over which the curtain had not been drawn as the flat was on the raised first floor and impossible to see into. She sat and stared out into the night and the hazy stars of light from the tower block, and let the music of the ballet carry her away in little jolts. She was thinking how she must get up and jam the door with a chair before she went to sleep, when the dark shape of a man tumbled past her window. It was followed a breath later by a woman's hollow scream soaring up from the basement where the body had landed with a thud. Lisa twisted the dial to cut off the sound of the television, and sat paralysed on the edge of the bed, wondering how it was that the woman had managed to climb down so quickly into the basement. It was possible that she had also fallen, and Lisa had simply failed to notice her as she fluttered by. The woman screamed again, the razor edges of her voice grazing the window and rattling the loose lock of the door. Lisa put on her shoes and a coat, and, leaving the flat door open for a quick re-entry, crept softly down the stairs.

A small crowd of familiar faces hovered on the street. No one spoke above a whisper and there were glints of intrigue and dread in the eyes that she met. Lisa was reminded of the uneasy feeling of her first Guy Fawkes'.

Steen had climbed down past the spikes and spears of the basement railings and was crouching near the woman with a blanket and a string of soothing words. The woman lay, half burying the man with her body, where he had fallen stretched out on his back in the damp and litter of the basement yard.

Lisa saw Heidi standing, smoking, by her staircase. She was wearing a pink padded dressing-gown. 'He fell right past my window,' Lisa told her, and then had to cover her face with both hands to stop the grin that was spreading from taking control of her face.

The inhabitants of Peerless Flats shuffled aimlessly. No one felt they could leave before the ambulance arrived. 'Did he jump?' someone asked in a whisper, and then another voice, incredulous, 'He jumped? Why did he jump?' The man on crutches from the fourth floor who had descended the stairs, despite pyjamas and his disability, told them in an authoritative voice, 'He didn't jump. He was trying to break in.'

'That's no burglar,' Heidi interrupted, 'that's Jim, he lives at number 56, he probably just forgot his key,' and everyone nodded as if this was an explanation they could readily accept.

The ambulance took longer than usual to arrive. Someone had had to run up to the payphone on the Old
Street roundabout to dial 999, as not one person in the
flats owned a telephone. It was a steadfast show of faith
in the temporariness of their accommodation. When the
ambulance did arrive, a woman in the basement allowed
the men to bring the stretcher in through her bay
window, saving them the struggle of hauling his body up
to street level by pulley.

Lisa slipped back upstairs. The door to her flat was
open and the tiny black figures of the dancers continued
to leap and scatter across the screen.

The moment Lisa woke the next morning she regretted
not having gone to the country with her mother. She felt
so lonely she could hardly bring herself to get out of bed.
She considered visiting Ruby. Ruby's hospital was on
the outskirts of London, but without a car she didn't
know if it was possible to get there. Anyway, the last
time they had been to see her, Ruby was so busy she
could barely spare the time for a cup of tea. She had a
boyfriend in the men's ward on the other side of the
hospital, and she had a date with him that afternoon at
the AA disco. Ruby told Lisa that her boyfriend was
from Liverpool. He was dead handsome, she said, and
addicted to a specific brand of cough mixture.

Lisa thought of ringing Sarah. She hadn't seen her
since New Year, but the possibility of Tom picking up
the phone and demanding to know the whereabouts of
Ruby decided her against it. She struggled free of the
sheets that had tangled cold and clammy round her feet

and went to look out of the window. She half expected to see a man's white outline spreadeagled on the ground below, but the only sign of the night before was the abundance of cigarette butts trodden into the pavement. Janey, Lisa thought. She could ring Janey. And then she remembered Janey was away. She was staying with her Gran, who had a caravan near Newhaven.

Lisa went through to the kitchen. She opened the fridge, and, overcome with a sudden pang of hunger, took out her icy plate of rice. She had wrapped the food in a sheet of clingfilm and now she swivelled the plate in her hands to check that the sealed edges had not been disturbed. She placed it on the table and turned it slowly round, bracing herself for the moment when she would tear off the wrapping and lift a stacked forkful of food into her mouth, but, as she peeled back the edges of the clingfilm, her stomach began to claw and tighten and a wave of fear drove her appetite away. It left her reeling, so that in a moment of despair she lay down on the kitchen floor and let her mouth fill up with tears. 'The worst thing that could happen is that I die,' she said, over and over to herself, but she knew it was not the worst thing that could happen, and even if it was, it was of little comfort.

She continued to lie on the floor. Maybe it was lucky Janey was away in Newhaven. She imagined what she would say if she were to confide in her. She could hear the strain of envy in her voice. 'Just think, you'll be able to use this in your acting!' Despite herself this made Lisa laugh and she scrambled up from the floor and peeled and ate a banana, gulping it down before she had a moment to scare herself off.

Lisa was frantic to come up with someone she could

visit. Her father, and a girl called Buzz she had once met at a bus stop, were the only people she could think of. She remembered her father peering at her in the darkness, shifting from foot to foot and waiting for her to go away, and she opted for Buzz. She had had a letter from her some months before saying she was living alone in a Volkswagen van in a field outside Tonbridge. She had invited Lisa to visit. 'Just turn up. Any time.' There was a list of directions. Lisa searched frantically for the letter. Get a train from Charing Cross, she remembered that. She could remember the rhythm of the directions but not the actual words. Get a train from Charing Cross, get off at Tonbridge, walk into the tum te tum — the town centre? the bus station? Get the number something bus, up a hill, across a bridge, get off, climb over a gate and there's the field. Get the number 9 bus? The number 19 bus? The 92? Lisa felt confident the number would reveal itself to her. The train journey might jog it into place. She gave up on her search for the letter and prepared to be away for up to a week. She packed a bag and left a note for her mother.

Tonbridge was in Kent and the train took just under an hour. Lisa spent the entire journey matching buses with numbers until she began to feel sick with the effort. She decided that once she got off the train everything would come back to her. She started to convince herself that she had made this journey before. That she would know her way to the tobacconist and the sweetshop and the park in the centre of town, like a man in a film she had once seen with Greer Garson. The man, who had lost his memory during the war, was astounded to find he knew his way around a sleepy, sepia-coloured village. It emerged that it was the village he had been born in and where his wife, not his fiancée Greer Garson but a plain woman with a bun, still lived.

When Lisa handed in her ticket with a thin crowd of commuters and was squeezed out into the station fore-court, there was nothing in sight that looked even re-motely familiar. She stood dolefully on the concrete strip of pavement and wondered which road she should take off the railway bridge that faced her. There wasn't a bus in sight. The people who had travelled with her dis-appeared into taxis and waiting cars and were sped away. Lisa asked the ticket collector the way to the centre of town, and was pointed wordlessly down the sharp slope of a hill where almost immediately she came upon a bus stop. Her heart leapt as she scanned the timetable, but there were so many buses listed and with such foreign-sounding destinations that she felt sure it couldn't be the right stop. Lisa turned away and continued to walk down the hill, which soon evened out into a straight high street of shops, chemists and bakers and building societies, all closed up for the night. In the distance she could see that the road twisted away out of sight by the side of a tall building. And then she felt sure she remembered. 'Get off the train, go *down* a hill, round a corner, and there will be a bus.' She repeated this to herself over and over as she walked, frightened that these valuable directions would slip away now that she'd finally got a hold of them. But when she reached the point where the road curved, she found she had to cross a wooden bridge over a wide and noisy river, and on the other side, around the corner, there was not a bus, but the ruins of a dimly lit medieval castle that no one, no one at all, could forget to mention.

Lisa turned abruptly and began to walk back the way

she'd come. She wanted to stop and ask one of the people hurrying by, holding their coats shut against the light rain, but she didn't know what she could ask. She kept walking until she had walked right out through the other side of the town. She walked past a church with a clock on its tower whose hands shivered as it struck the hour, and along the grass verge of two roundabouts with signs for Hastings, Sevenoaks and Maidstone. The road sloped up in a hill, with high, dark hedges on either side. It was possible this might be the hill Buzz had meant in her letter, but if it was the hill with the field off it, then why would she have told her to catch a bus? The street lights stopped at this point and the hill, with its overgrown hedges, lay shrouded in an eerie night. Lisa traced her way back towards the church. There was a pub on a corner with warm, orange light seeping through its windows. She imagined Buzz sitting inside with a pint of bitter and a table covered with half-ounce packets of Golden Virginia, Rizla papers and cheese-and-onion crisps. She longed to see her smiling, freckled face, and her twinkling eyes clogged almost shut with mascara. She imagined her at a table of men all vying for attention.

Lisa went over to the pub and peered through a window. The glass was knobbled and frosted and gave nothing away. She was about to edge her way through the doors into the lounge bar when a roaring contingent of bikers skidded to a halt in the car park and began to dismount. Lisa flattened herself against the wall of the porch and, as they spiked and steadied their bikes, she slipped away around the side of the pub. Once on the safety of the road, she resumed her walk back into the town centre.

The town was almost utterly deserted now. She stared wistfully into the faces of the occasional passers-by. Mostly young couples wandering aimlessly hand in hand. There was no one scruffy or wild enough to look as if they were a friend of Buzz's. Eventually Lisa found another bus stop and studied the timetable. There was a 209, which sounded hopeful, and a 29, but they had both stopped running shortly before eight. Lisa clutched the return ticket lying deep in the bottom of her pocket, and headed for the station. The last train to London didn't leave until ten to ten and she sat down on a bench to wait. 'Something good has to happen,' she told herself. The more she thought about it the more convinced she became that something good really would have to happen. And she knew what it was going to be. She would meet someone on the train. Someone with whom she could mark this day as the beginning of the rest of her life. Someone to fall in love with. She scrabbled in her bag until she found the mirror that had come as a free gift Sellotaped to a tube of Nivea cream. It was so tiny that she could only see small parts of her face at a time. She inspected her right eye and applied a line of black eyeliner. Ruby, who had recently taken to wearing no makeup whatsoever except a perfect arc of bright red lipstick, said it was seventies and out of date to wear eyeliner. Lisa guiltily applied another smudge of black to her left eye. She had never mastered the art of lipstick. Her lips didn't seem to have a defined beginning or end, and lipstick, unless applied by an expert like Marlene, turned her face into that of a beaten-up fairground clown.

Lisa had to wait for nearly an hour before the London train pulled in. There was no one else waiting to get on apart from a smart woman who had arrived by taxi with less than a minute to spare. Lisa followed her on, attracted by her bustle and the spirit of her late arrival.

Once on the train Lisa was torn between the smoking carriage and the next compartment where the lady had seated herself and was fingering through a slick pile of magazines. There was no one in the smoking carriage except a man in a suit who had fallen asleep with his stomach hanging out of his shirt, and a boy who was listening to a handmade radio and rolling cigarettes from dog-ends that he picked up from the floor.

Lisa went through to the next carriage and sat diagonally opposite the woman. She stared at her own reflection in the glass and pretended to be looking through the window. Eventually she summoned up enough courage to ask the woman, 'Can I look at one of your magazines?' and the shock of her voice made them both jump. The woman looked up without enthusiasm. 'Help yourself,' she said.

As the train rumbled uneventfully through the black night and on into the London suburbs, Lisa had to accept that it was unlikely now anything was going to occur to change this day from the failure that it was.

She kept her head down as she wandered out into the little town of Charing Cross station with its newsagents and its cafés and its resident tramps. She was ashamed to be here again so soon and she resolved to tear up and burn the optimistic note she had left for her mother earlier that day.

Lisa spent the next few days alone at the flat, living off bowls of muesli that she sieved meticulously in order to examine each raisin, nut and sunflower seed. She stirred it up with water so that she wouldn't have to leave the house even for a pint of milk.

She hoped against hope that someone would break in on her seclusion, but when one night footsteps did stop on the stairs, and a hand rattled the letter-box, shaking the door so that it swayed and buckled on its hinges, Lisa was too ashamed to answer. 'Hello,' she heard Steen's thick voice, 'is anyone in there?' And she buried her face under the covers and held her breath until he went away.

The day Marguerite was due to return, Lisa decided she would have to leave the flat, if only for a short time, or her mother might suspect that there was something wrong. She cleaned and tidied all the rooms, leaving just enough mess to look as if she were alive: an ashtray, a half-drunk cup of tea, a small pile of discarded clothes. She dressed carefully in a red silk dress, which was large and hung in pleats from a belted waist, and put on a pair of white tights to disguise the fragility of her legs. She stood in front of the bathroom mirror and applied pale powdery rouge to her cheeks, remembering Marlene's tricks and makeup hints, and dabbing at her nose, her forehead and her chin to create a rosy glow. She brushed her hair and tied it back behind her ears with a shoelace. She was going to visit Ruby.

She asked the ticket inspector at Old Street for directions, and took a series of trains across London, arriving at the gates of Hanworth Hospital a little before midday.

Ruby was having her lunch. She was lying on her bed, picking the apple crumble from under a thick layer of yellow custard. She offered Lisa a loaded spoon. Lisa closed her eyes and swallowed.

'You're looking great,' Ruby told her.

Lisa shrugged and forced a smile.

Ruby finished up her pudding. Her short hair had grown out of its spikes and lay in soft waves against her head, framing her face so that her eyes shone dark and velvety.

They exchanged the usual family news.

'How's Mum?'

'Fine.'

'Seen Dad?'

'Yes.'

'Max?' Ruby asked, and Lisa began to tell her how he had recently become obsessed with the idea of shark-fishing in Hampstead Ponds and sometimes forgot all about foxes for up to an hour at a time, until she remembered that ultimately it bored Ruby to hear these stories and she switched the subject.

'Ruby . . .' She stretched out on her bed. 'Are you nearly cured?'

'Cured?' Ruby giggled. 'In here? You must be joking! Anyway, it's all right for me, I don't have a problem, it's not as if I were an addict or anything.'

Lisa looked at her hard to glimpse even the faintest shadow of a doubt, but Ruby looked back open-faced.

'So why did you have yourself admitted?' Lisa wanted to know.

Ruby rolled over on the bed, making room for Lisa to crawl up beside her so that her head rested on the same high hospital pillow. 'Promise you won't tell?'

Lisa nodded. She felt like a child again. Ruby's little sister.

'It wasn't the drugs,' she lowered her voice. 'It was Marlene.'

'Oh.' Lisa made a face to show she understood.

'She wouldn't let me out of the house. She said she was in love with me.'

'Oh,' Lisa said again. She tried to imagine Janey, or Sarah, or anyone she knew, saying anything like that to her.

'But do you like it in here?'

Ruby smiled and drew a deep, contented sigh. 'It's not bad.' Then she added ruefully, 'But they're talking about discharging me.'

'When?'

'I don't know. Soon.'

'What will you do?'

Ruby didn't answer.

'You could go back to Belgravia?'

'Yeah, I suppose . . .' Ruby turned on her side to face her. 'Listen, why don't you come and stay there with me?'

Lisa caught her breath. 'Do you mean it?' And then she remembered her mother and the long, laborious meeting she had sat through at the New Swift Housing Co-op, all so she could get a house with three bedrooms to make a home for her and Max. 'I'll have to see,' she said.

Ruby frowned minutely.

'It's just that Mum thinks there's a chance we might get housed and if I'm not there –'

'Don't worry yourself about it,' Ruby interrupted her. 'Anyway, Dad said he might send me away somewhere to recover.'

'Like where?'

'I don't know. Somewhere far from temptation. Kenya or the West Indies, or maybe Argentina.'

Lisa didn't know what to say. 'But what about your boyfriend with the cough mixture?'

'Oh him, he discharged himself, and anyway, I won't be gone for ever.'

Ruby had to meet Christine for some kind of therapeutic activity in another wing of the hospital. 'Sorry,' she said. 'If I'd known you were coming . . .' Ruby walked Lisa out into the grounds and hugged her good-bye. She hugged her very tightly so that a little strangled noise like a sigh came up from inside her chest. 'I keep thinking, since I've been in here, how I used to bully you when we were kids.'

For a horrible moment Lisa thought Ruby might be going to cry. She pulled away so she could see her face. 'I didn't mind, Ruby please don't think about it. I promise, really I promise, I didn't mind.'

Lisa sat in the smoking carriage, chain-smoking John Player Specials and thinking: She didn't bully me, she never bullied me. She thought of Ruby's fiery, uniformed figure racing through the playground, creating waves of anguish in anyone who crossed her, teachers and pupils alike. She smiled to think of Ruby's long, straight hair hanging almost to her waist, and the transfer stickers she liked to wear tattooed across her chest. A friend of their mother's had once reported having seen her on the main road, perched like Loki on the top of a battered pram, while Lisa, struggling and gasping and stretching her arms to reach the pram's high handle, attempted to push her at a befittingly violent pace. What the woman had failed to understand was that it was an honour to push Ruby. An honour she would have defied anyone at all to refuse.

After Ruby left the school, Lisa continued to live on, steeped in the glorious memory of her reign, and when new people arrived in the area, Lisa noted how they treated her with interest and sometimes even made attempts to gain her friendship, but she could never quite forgive them their state of ignorance, and always held them at a distance and even in some small contempt for not knowing, or having ever known, that she was in fact Ruby's little sister.

Lisa was so caught up in her reverie that she changed trains at the wrong station and found herself heading north towards Cockfosters. She jumped out at Finsbury Park, just as the doors were closing, and managed to avoid being rushed on along the Piccadilly Line. She found a map against a wall of the station and began to retrace her route. The map was at a point between two tunnels that led south and north away from the station platforms, and as she stood and calculated the shortest possible journey home, a familiar figure momentarily blotted out the arch of distant light and stepped into the strip-lit gloom of the tunnel. At one glance she knew that it was Quentin. She recognized his swagger and the way he walked with his shoulders back. He sauntered towards her down the gradual underground slope. Lisa continued to stare at the map so hard that it blurred in front of her eyes, and all the time over her right shoulder she could see the dark outline of Quentin as he approached. She heard his breathing as he swayed past, turned the corner and headed in the direction of the trains. 'Quentin,' she called, surprise in her voice, as if she had just seen him, and he turned around and surveyed her calmly as he continued to walk backwards. Lisa ran towards him. She could tell he hadn't recognized her and she took it as a compliment. She smiled up into his face. 'Quentin,' she said, 'it's me. Lisa.' Quentin looked at her for so long, with his brown eyes creased up like a Hollywood photograph and his head tilted a little to one side, that Lisa began to pray for lightning or a sudden fatal heart attack to release her from the mortification of his stare.

Finally he smiled. 'Where the hell have you been?' he said, in a voice pressed down with gentleness, and with an arm around her shoulder he began to walk with her back along the sloping tunnel.

'Weren't you on your way somewhere?' Lisa asked him, but he said nothing. When they got to the concrete ridge which was the stop for the W7 bus he put his arms around her waist and kissed her. He lifted her off the ground and held her hard against him. 'You disappeared,' he said. 'How did you do that?'

Lisa was so happy she felt like lying down to die. She sat next to Quentin on the top deck, at the very front, and let herself be jolted and rattled against him by the movement of the bus. They got off at the top of the hill where they could see the spire and dome of Alexandra Palace on the peak of the next rise, and between them the valley of brick houses with their gardens and hedges and wooden sheds and the streets that wound down into the village of Crouch End. They walked back down the hill to Quentin's house and he kept hold of her hand as they climbed up the three flights of stairs to his flat on the top floor. Lisa sat on the edge of the thin, covered mattress that was Quentin's bed and the only place in the room to sit, and waited for him while he made tea in the kitchen. She arranged the folds of her dress, one by one, so that they covered her legs and hung like shiny red ribbons almost to her feet. She felt her pulse and counted her toes and tried to keep her mind occupied while she waited for him to reappear. It was late afternoon and the sun was setting somewhere over Finsbury Park, throwing a pale and yellow winter light in through the windows of the room.

Quentin reappeared with two mugs of tea. He placed them by the edge of the bed and put a record on the record player. 'D'you like this guy?' he asked her, and Lisa nodded as the first slow beats of an unfamiliar song filled the room. She reached for her tea to hide her ignorance, but before she could bring it to her lips, Quentin was kneeling over her. 'Leave that,' he whispered and he kept his hand on her arm while she replaced the cup. He sank on to the bed and pulled her down with him so that all the carefully arranged pleats of her dress flew into a ruffled mass of silk. Lisa smiled at him. She wanted him to say, 'I love you,' or, 'I've missed you,' or even, 'It's nice seeing you again,' but when she looked into his eyes he just sighed and closed them and, with his hands on her back, he twisted her round so that she lay pressed above him, hard against his chest.

Quentin loosened her belt and slipped open the zip that ran along her left side. He lifted the dress up over her head with one strong sweep of his hands. Lisa lay back in her white tights. She was still unused to the changed appearance of her body and, for the sake of inhibition and the day, she decided she may as well give in to being someone else and allow him to make love to her without a shiver of restraint.

Quentin woke with a start. Lisa had been watching him, propped up on one elbow while he slept. 'Fucking shite,' he said, leaping out of bed. 'What time is it, anyway?'

Lisa didn't know. It was dark and she had been thinking vaguely for some time that she should get up and go home to see her mother and Max who would have returned by now. Quentin rummaged through the discarded clothes strewn across the floor, throwing them into the air as he searched wildly for the clock. 'Jesus God,' he cursed when he found it, 'it's nearly ten. I'll be lucky to get there by closing time.'

Lisa found her dress half buried down the side of the mattress. She pulled it on and stood up in the hope the creases might fall out. Quentin railed around the room looking for his keys, his comb, his cigarettes, his various packets of drugs, and all the while cursing in what Lisa could only assume was a mood of sour regret. She slipped on her shoes, and with her coat over her arm waited dutifully by the door.

Once they were out on the street he took her hand. 'Where are you heading?' he asked.

'Home.'

Quentin nodded. 'I'm going the other way.' He hugged her and she kept her shoulders stiff and straight like Max. 'If you ever feel like calling round' – he looked back up at the windows of his flat – 'don't forget the bells don't work. Just shout' – Lisa softened by way of thanks – 'and I'll be there.' He grinned as if to say: You believe that and you'll believe anything.

'How could you believe me when I told you that I loved you when you know I've been a liar all my life,' Lisa hummed to herself as she walked away. Quentin was waiting at a bus stop on the other side of the road. She could see him under a street lamp, sitting on the wall smoking a cigarette. She waved at him just before the road curved out of sight, but he didn't see her.

Lisa walked on, her mind full of the weight of Quentin's hands. He had stroked her back, running his fingers up the ridge of her spine and cradling the base of her skull in his palm so that her eyes began to soften and she was able to return his kisses without breaking sharply off for air. It was only when he forced himself inside her that she lost the thread of his sweetness, and the domed rooms inside her head filled up with people, leering and scrambling and talking over each other in harsh and whispery voices. All she could do was fight them off and wait for it to be over. She didn't blame Quentin. Afterwards she had lain against his warm back and tried not to wake him with the shaking of her body and the little gasps that rattled out of her ribs when she breathed.

Once Lisa emerged above ground at Old Street roundabout, she was filled with such a longing to see her mother that she broke into a run. She ran at top speed to make up for the time lost in taking the long way round. She had intended risking the mournful echo of the short cut, but a sudden stab of happiness had resulted in a decision in favour of her safety.

Lisa could see streams of light spilling out around the warped edges of the door as she sped up the last flight of

166

stairs. Rather than search her pockets for a key, she flapped the letter-box and called in her impatience to be let in.

Marguerite swung open the door. 'Where have you been?' Her eyes were fierce. Her face was flushed with anger. 'I've been sitting here waiting for you since six.' She held the door half closed against her like a shield. 'I was on the verge of calling the police.'

'I'm sorry.' Lisa winced against the loudness of her mother's voice and attempted to slink into the room. 'I'm sorry, I didn't think . . .'

'But it's so unlike you,' Marguerite accused. 'It's just so unlike you to be thoughtless.' She slammed the door shut, and then, remembering, put a finger to her lips. Lisa glanced through into the bedroom where Max was sleeping on the top bunk, his arms and legs flailed out as if he had been drugged mid-bout in a wrestling match. Marguerite walked through to the kitchen and sank down at the table. 'Well, you're home.' And, heaving her voice on to a lighter note, she added, 'Tell me, have you been having a lovely time?'

Lisa took off her coat, revealing the disarray of her mother's red dress. 'Yes,' she said, 'I have.'

Marguerite leant close in to her. She was looking into the very centre of her eyes. 'I'm going to have to ask you something.' She took a breath and swallowed. Lisa looked at the floor. She imagined her mother had decided that this was the moment to explain the facts of life to her. Mum, she wanted to say, don't you think it's a bit late for that? But Marguerite twisted and pulled at her hands. 'Steen seems to think you've been taking drugs, hard drugs. He mentioned something about heroin.' She looked as if she were about to cry.

Lisa was so surprised she laughed out loud. 'Don't be silly!' She shook her head and raised her hands. 'You don't need to worry about me, I promise.' Lisa watched as the visible signs of relief smoothed out the lines around her mother's mouth. 'What does Steen know, anyway?'

Marguerite apologized. 'It wasn't that I believed him, but you can understand that I had to ask.'

'Of course I do,' Lisa said, 'but really, I'm fine.'

Marguerite told Lisa about her time away and all the people who had asked after her, wanting to know how she was getting on at college. She said there wasn't anyone who didn't remark on the extraordinary resemblance between Max and his father. 'As long as it's just physical,' Marguerite smiled. She heated up the vegetable soup that sat on the stove and Lisa ate, keeping her eyes pinned to her mother's face as the lentils and tiny pasta rings she used as stock slipped down her throat.

Lisa went around to Heidi to ask for the name and address of the doctor she had mentioned some months ago who tested for allergies. Her mother's interrogation, misguided as it was, had left her with a sense of having narrowly escaped, and she resolved to find herself a cure before it was too late. To cover her tracks, she said it was possible she might be allergic to oysters. Heidi laughed and wrote out the details on a scrap of paper. 'You'll live,' she said, and she continued to scrub at the nappies that had been soaking overnight in the kitchen sink.

Lisa made an appointment to see the doctor, whose surgery was on Baker Street. She attempted to explain her symptoms to him, but he stopped her with a cynical smile, and ordered her to hold out her right arm at an angle. He then placed, one at a time, various small objects in her palm and pushed down heavily on her wrist to check the strength of her resistance. Momentarily he thought she might be suffering from mercury poisoning, and became quite animated as he explained how all the fillings in her teeth would have to be replaced at some great expense to herself, but her arm defied his diagnosis and continued to resist his weight as he pushed down on her wrist. Eventually he was forced to admit that this could not be the case and, after twenty more minutes in which she handled substances ranging from iridium to an Earl Grey tea bag, he informed her that she was allergic to nothing at all except perfume. Something of which she was already aware.

Lisa was so disappointed tears welled up in her eyes as she wrote out her cheque. She was able to draw on some money that she had in a bank account, placed there the previous year as a present from her father. It hurt her to chip away from it. Ruby had taken hers out the same week and spent it on clothes and taxis and edible delicacies from the Harrods Food Hall, but Lisa would have been happy never to disturb her share, leaving it for ever safe inside the bank as a calm green reminder of her father.

The doctor packed her cheque away in a small drawer and suggested that her symptoms might be the result of tension. Lisa disagreed. You'd be feeling tense if you'd just paid thirty pounds to be told something you already know, she thought, but she said nothing. The doctor referred her to an acupuncturist and made an appointment for her there and then for the following week.

The acupuncturist was a Mr Bunzl and was unusually tall with the bone structure of an actor born to play Frankenstein. He led Lisa into a partitioned room with a disproportionately high ceiling and told her to remove her clothes. Without another word he retreated through a flimsy door in the far wall and shut himself out with a faint shudder of the plasterboard. A small heater blew hot air into the draught under the window, and as it was the only heating in the room, Lisa stood in front of it as she undressed. It boiled her legs up to the knee and left the rest of her body quivering with goose bumps. She was in a quandary as to whether or not to remove her vest, regretting miserably that she had not thought to wear her one and only bra. She kept on her knickers and with one arm across her chest climbed on to the high bed that stood alone in the centre of the room. She lay face up under the white cotton cover and waited.

It seemed an eternity before the acupuncturist reappeared. When he did, Lisa said before she could stop herself, 'I hope it's all right I'm not wearing a bra?'

Mr Bunzl looked away and, pushing her question aside with lowered eyebrows, pulled up a chair. He wanted to know the history and precise nature of Lisa's ailment.

Lisa talked as if to the ceiling. She stuck to a strictly physical description of the state of her mind and laid bare the crackling and snapping of her bones. She tried to explain the sensation of cold burning that had descended on her in the strip-lit corridor, and how it was necessary to cover the top of her head with her hand to stop her mind escaping like an icicle. She laughed at her descriptions as she talked, her eyes fixed on the plaster rose in the centre of the ceiling. She laughed to reassure Mr Bunzl that she was not mad. She glanced over to gauge his reaction, but he continued to nod darkly and scribble notes on to a sheet of paper. She omitted to tell him about the violent fear she was seized with and the secret measures to which she would go to save herself from being poisoned. She forgot to mention the slow ebb of her period and the way her throat closed up in panic each time she raised a fork to her mouth.

To Lisa's surprise he didn't stick any needles into her but folded his pad and told her to get dressed. He remained in the room with his face turned to the wall, intent on the scrawl of her case. Lisa dressed quickly. She felt dizzy from having spoken her thoughts aloud in sentences for the first time, and, now that she was safely

dressed and out of danger of his needles, a wall of disappointment engulfed her. She had expected her confidence
to incite him into action. She had imagined he might
stick a needle somewhere in her spine and with a hiss
draw the trouble out, leaving her soft and quiet. A child
again. But he had done nothing.

Mr Bunzl crossed the room quietly. He bent his knees
to avoid towering so much over her and pressed his
fingertips together, bringing his hands close up to her
face. 'I am pressing the nail of each finger into the tip of
the soft pad of the fingers on the other hand.' It was
exactly what he was doing and Lisa brought her hands
up to match his. 'I want you to do this each morning
and each evening for five minutes. It doesn't matter
where you press.' Mr Bunzl went on to list all the places
in which you could practise pressing the pads of your
fingers. 'The bed, the bath, the bus . . . Five minutes
with one hand, and then five minutes with the other.
This will take away the tension in the head, and all will
be well.'

His fee was fifteen pounds and he made an appointment for Lisa to come and see him again in two weeks'
time. 'Keep pressing,' he said, holding his hands up at
her in a spidery prayer as she left.

Lisa's disappointment had turned to an edge of despair. She dragged her feet as she walked away from the
gloom of his surgery. She would follow his daily instructions, she knew, she was too superstitious not to, and
even return for her next appointment, but she was unable
to believe that the simple pressing of her fingertips would
cure her.

Lisa had become so quiet at college that she suspected she would hardly be missed if she failed to turn up. It was Monday morning and the week started with a class in movement improvisation. It was a class that always succeeded in embarrassing Lisa into virtual immobility.

'What are you? A tree?' the teacher had barked at her on more than one occasion.

Lisa clung to the idea that this, surely, had nothing to do with being a real actress. The kind of actress who toured the country in classic plays that involved wearing bustles and corsets and elaborate hats. She pressed her fingers together and decided to take the morning off. She could visit Ruby and use the hour of the journey to contemplate Quentin and a course of action. She still had the excuse of retrieving her ring. She had seen it in his bathroom, lying forgotten in a soap dish. It was dull and discoloured and, she decided, more valuable where it was.

When Lisa arrived at the hospital, Ruby was about to have her bath. 'I'll smuggle you in,' she said.

First Ruby had to apply for a plug. 'Special privilege,' she winked.

None of the baths in Hanworth Hospital had plugs. Or taps. 'No unsupervised bathing,' Ruby explained, and when Lisa continued to look confused, 'so you can't drown yourself, muggins.' She threw her the cold tap to screw on.

Ruby let the bath fill up to the very top so that when she got in, a layer of water slid off and splashed on to the floor. Lisa sat on a chair and watched her. She couldn't think of a thing to say. 'How's Christine?' she asked at length.

Ruby was lathering her hair. 'Killing for a drink,' and she laughed dementedly and slid her head under the water. When she shot back up, her eyes streaming and her hair sleek and rinsed, Lisa noticed that the row of dark blue scars that ran in dots along her inside arm were beginning to fade. 'Have I got fat?' Ruby asked suspiciously, seeing herself watched, and Lisa denied it vigorously.

Lisa pressed her fingertips together. She wanted to see if Ruby would recognize what it was she was doing. For all she knew, it was a well-known cure. Ruby gave her hair a second wash, sank under the water and said nothing.

When Lisa arrived back at Peerless Street, a man was standing talking to Heidi in the entrance to the flats. As Lisa approached they shook hands and she heard Heidi murmur her congratulations.

'Who was that?' Lisa asked. Heidi lowered her voice, 'It's Jim,' and she nodded in the direction of the basement yard.

'Jim?' She looked up at her window. 'The man who forgot his key? But I thought he —'

'Shh.' Heidi raised her finger to her lips and continued in a stage whisper, 'It's a miracle what people survive.' They stood and watched him as he walked to the end of

Peerless Street and disappeared through a side door of the local pub. 'By the way,' Heidi said, 'did you ever see that doctor about the allergy to oysters?'

Lisa froze on the bottom step. 'No, I couldn't be bothered.' And she ran on up the stairs without another word.

For the next two weeks Lisa pressed her fingertips together at every opportunity. She assumed it was better to press too often than not to press often enough, and she listened warily for any changes. Much as she had suspected, there were none.

The evening before she was due to go back to see Mr Bunzl, Lisa discovered Tom lounging against a wall in the foyer of her college reading a copy of a weekly magazine. He was very excited. Someone had compiled a list of the ten men they would most like to have a night of passion with and Tom's name featured on it, eighth. Tom thrust the magazine into Lisa's hands. 'Do you know her? Who is she? Where has she been all my life?' he demanded.

The list had been compiled by a girl called Emilia Hilton. She had a mass of bleached hair piled on top of her head like Debbie Harry, but her face was so over-exposed that, apart from two round, bright eyes, she appeared to have no other features. Lisa stared at the girl's name as if she might be able to dredge up some familiarity with her, even though she could have told Tom straight away that she wouldn't know. 'I've got to meet her,' Tom said when she eventually admitted to her ignorance. He stuffed the rolled magazine into the back pocket of his jeans and asked if she wanted to come for a drink.

They walked through the housing estates that stretched away towards King's Cross to where the college pub stood in a paved-over square with two stinking benches and several trees that waved and shivered in their wire encasements. 'I'll come for one drink,' Lisa said, 'but then I'll have to go.' It was Max's sixth birthday and a tea party was being held in his honour. Tom bought himself a pint of Guinness and a Bell's, and insisted Lisa have the same. Lisa obediently drained her whisky but was unable to stomach the froth of the thick and bitter Guinness. Tom obligingly drank it for her and went to the bar to reorder. After the third round he took out the magazine and held it up to the light. He gazed into the startled eyes of the girl whose list he was on. 'I'm in love,' he said in a voice thick with whisky and emotion. 'I'm in love and I've got to find you, if it's the last thing I do,' and he staggered to the bar to put in his order for another round.

Each time Lisa made a move to leave, Tom caught her wrist and forced her back on to the seat beside him. 'Just stay for one more,' he insisted, his grey eyes threatening to overflow. By now there were so many glasses on their table that to attempt to get out from behind it was a daunting prospect.

'I've really got to go,' Lisa mumbled, closing her eyes, and then forcing them open again fast as the spin inside her head began to pick up speed.

'No, no, you can't,' Tom pleaded, and, in an effort to grab hold of her, he tipped Guinness over the out-stretched pages of the magazine, so that, as they watched, the face of Tom's dream-girl dissolved into a thin and papery mess. Tom tried desperately to save the picture by peeling it off in one go, but the weight of the Guinness glued it to the table top and it fell apart in his hands. In a last, desperate attempt to capture even a fraction of the article, Tom succeeded in knocking over the remains of his pint so that the table became a dark sea of matchsticks and cigarette butts, an occasional piece of sodden type floating on its overflowing surface. Lisa looked up to see the barman scowling over at them, and before Tom could topple the whole table as he grabbed at the floating letters of his name, Lisa hoisted him up and, with some difficulty, manoeuvred him towards the door.

'Come and have some tea at our house,' she insisted. And arm in arm they staggered towards the station.

Max's tea party was almost over when they arrived at Peerless Flats. Max was eating chocolate fingers through the visor of his plastic helmet and shouting orders to foxes that hovered in the corners of the room. Marguerite, Heidi and Steen were smoking in the kitchen.

The moment Max saw Tom, he charged him as if he were simply continuing the battle begun on New Year's Eve. Tom threw himself on to the bed to avoid being butted by the hard top of his helmet, and pleaded with Max for mercy. 'I'm feeling a little fragile,' he said, covering his head with his hands and giggling uncontrollably. 'If you don't stop, I'm liable to throw up all over you.' Max roared with delight. He jumped up and down on the bed so that the springs whined and sang and threatened to snap. Tom's long, thin body heaved with the motion. Lisa went through to the kitchen to make coffee.

'I'm sorry I'm so late,' she said.

'It's all right.' Marguerite looked at her proudly and smiled.

'Best years of your life,' Steen said, and he raised his glass.

A low groan of agony rose up from the other room. Tom, clutching his stomach, and closely followed by

Max, pushed his way through the kitchen, stumbling over discarded toys and the legs of chairs and fumbling his way blind towards the toilet. Marguerite and Heidi began to laugh. 'Best years of your life,' Steen said again, and Lisa ran the cold tap furiously to drown out the sound of his vomiting.

Lisa lay under the white sheet on the high bed of Mr Bunzl's practice. 'It didn't work,' she told him flatly, when he asked how she was feeling.

Mr Bunzl was astounded. His mammoth hands fluttered and the heavy bones of his face seemed ready to collapse. Lisa fixed her eyes on the ceiling and tried to keep her heart hard against him as she traced the skeletal cracks that rode across the plaster.

Mr Bunzl stacked her flimsy notes against his knee and placed them on a chair. 'I am going to use some needles,' he said in a voice so soothing as to send a chill through the air. Lisa didn't answer. She was fighting with a lump in her throat. 'Now breathe in,' Mr Bunzl instructed, 'and out.'

Lisa felt a tiny sting like the first bite of a bee before the poison takes effect. She wanted to look down to see the exact point of the tingling, but the acupuncturist had moved away from her feet and was instructing her to breathe slowly in and out while he placed two needles in the top of her head. She felt nothing but an itching around the jab of each pin.

Mr Bunzl placed six needles in various parts of her body and then stood over her as if he were monitoring the possibilities of an immediate reaction. 'Any pain?' he asked, and Lisa gulped and admitted that there was none.

Whether this was the right answer or not, Lisa wasn't

sure, for he then proceeded to busy himself about her prostrate body, placing small lumps of incense on the tip of each needle and setting light to them with a match. Lisa began to smoke like a funeral pyre. She was wreathed in a veil through which she could just make out the retreating figure of Mr Bunzl, side-stepping away from her, until with a click and a shudder of the wall he levered himself out through the partition door.

Lisa walked away from the surgery in a kind of trance. Her eyes felt soft in her head and her mouth was full of lullabies. She stopped at a parade of shops and bought three bunches of sweet white narcissi. She began to run. She ran past the gloomy entrance to the underground station and along a canal that stretched through Maida Vale and led up on to the start of Edgware Road. She leapt, the petals of her flowers flapping, on to the open back of a double-decker bus, and, as she squeezed herself inside and through the throng of people standing, an earlier memory than she had ever known burst in on her. She was running with her mother. They were running for a bus and, as the distances closed in, the grip on her hand tightened and her speed picked up and she was flying, flying out from her mother's arm as the whole world of the city blurred below her feet. She had trodden air with her shoes which were red like the bus, and, just when she thought she would slip out of her shoulder-blade and twist away through the trees, her mother's strong hand had swung her to safety and she had been lost among shopping-bags and the trouser legs of the conductor. She had waited breathless for the world to steady itself and catch her up.

Lisa pushed her way to the front of the bus and stood pressed against the driver's window. She closed her eyes and let her face hang over the honeysuckle centres of her flowers. Mr Bunzl had left her alone while the smoke from the incense thinned and formed itself into delicate plumes that rose in spirals to the ceiling. Lisa didn't know how long she had lain there, but she had become transfixed by the coils of smoke, soft as carded wool, and had forgotten her fury against the wasted weeks of pressing at her fingertips. She had been surprised by the reappearance of the acupuncturist, who moved around her wordlessly drawing out the needles. 'I will see you again in two weeks,' he said and Lisa had written out her cheque without a trace of bile.

Lisa stood her flowers in a glass of water, keeping them in their paper wrapping to give to Ruby on her Saturday visit. Marguerite was unable to go with her as it was the quarterly housing co-operative meeting, at which all new and homeless members were allowed to plead their case. Lisa was on the point of asking if she might take Max along for company, when Max announced from under the table that he had succeeded in making his eyeballs disappear.

'Look,' he screamed, sliding out along the kitchen floor, 'Lisa, see if you can do it too.'

Lisa covered her eyes with her hand.

'Goodbye,' she called, 'good luck,' and, feeling blindly for her coat, she promised to eat the apple her mother had pushed into her pocket.

When Lisa arrived at Ruby's ward, Ruby was not

there. Her bed was neatly made and was piled high with her belongings. Lisa squeezed herself between two cardboard boxes and waited. She was tempted to search through a bag to see if Ruby had remembered to pack the mother-of-pearl bracelet that had not been seen or mentioned since Christmas, but instead she drew the apple out of her pocket and inspected it. She turned it over and rubbed it on the sleeve of her coat. It was an English Pippin and not the kind of fruit that ever achieves a shine. There were little weather-beaten creases in its skin which Lisa peered into.

'What are you doing?' Ruby's voice startled her from across the ward.

'Nothing?' Lisa took a bite of the apple to prove she was not afraid.

'I'm leaving today,' Ruby sighed, sitting down beside her and leaning back against her bags.

Lisa nodded. 'That's right. I came to see you off.' She had in fact until this minute completely forgotten the details of her previous visit. Her head began to swim. 'Do you mean leaving, leaving the country? Where did you say you were going? To . . . to . . . ?' She took a bite out of her lip in her anxiety.

'Dad's taking me to lunch,' Ruby said calmly. 'Why don't you come?'

Their father arrived wearing a slate-grey trench coat. He had a newspaper rolled up under his arm and he tapped his foot and shifted edgily from side to side. 'I've got a bit of a bet on the two-thirty-five at Sandown Park,' he said. 'Shall we go?' They loaded Ruby's possessions into the boot of the car, a fat and roomy Rover with a severe dent in its left wing.

'What do you fancy?' He glanced into the back where Lisa was still clutching her fading bunch of flowers.

'Lobster,' Ruby said, 'and champagne!' She turned in her seat to watch as the receding mass of Hanworth Hospital twisted out of sight with a bend in the road.

Their father tapped his fingers on the steering-wheel. 'We could, we could,' but he wasn't committing himself.

'A pizza?' Lisa suggested, but he only tapped his tongue against the roof of his mouth.

It transpired he needed to be near a television.

'Why not go to the race course? Watch the horses run from there?' Ruby was not making her suggestion in all innocence, but with bravado and a challenge in her voice. Lisa leant forward so that her face was resting on the back of Ruby's seat. Their father kept his eyes on the road. 'It's an idea,' he mused.

'Is it because you win too often?' Lisa asked him.

Her father swerved into the inside lane to overtake a juggernaut. Lisa and Ruby both grasped the seat. 'Have you ever heard the term "debt of honour"?' He was back in the fast lane and sailing towards ninety.

'We could disguise you,' Ruby broke in. 'I've got clothes in the back.'

Lisa put her arms around her sister's neck and hugged her.

Their father, a thoughtful smile on his face, careered across the dual carriageway and pulled into a lay-by. 'Let's see what you've got,' he said.

Ruby heaved her bags out of the boot and began to rummage through the contents. Lisa ran back and forth catching at garments as they escaped in the tornado of the passing cars. She found a long, sequinned scarf lined with memories of Marlene which their father wrapped around his head and twisted into a turban. 'How do I look?' he asked, and he began to skip across the lay-by from side to side, his hands raised and flat in an Egyptian dance. Cars slowed visibly and Ruby and Lisa rocked on their heels. 'Try this?' Ruby hurled a navy blue beret into the wind and Lisa caught it and handed it over. The beret turned the trench coat into a soldier's uniform and created a sombre and menacing impression. 'All wrong,' they agreed and Ruby continued to rifle. Eventually she found what she was looking for and dragged a white cotton jacket up from the depths of her packing. It looked like a chef's coat with stiff collars and a long split up the back. Their father changed in an instant, throwing his own coat into the back seat of the car and transforming momentarily into Charlie Chaplin before the addition of Ruby's tinted glasses fixed him as an eccentric and mildly sinister Frenchman. Lisa broke the stem of a white narcissus and wove the flower through his buttonhole. 'That's it,' and they piled Ruby's luggage back into the boot.

There was less than twenty minutes before the race was due to start. 'Don't worry, we'll make it,' their father assured them as he sped his car against the traffic. He leapt up pavements, slipped through lights and overtook seamlessly from the inside, provoking a fanfare of disapproval from pedestrians and motorists alike. Once they were on to a clear stretch of road, he reached into the glove compartment and brought out a fat white envelope. He handed it to Ruby. Inside was a map of car parks and a cluster of pink cardboard badges with 'Members' stand' printed across them. 'Didn't think I'd be using these,' he said as he pushed the car through amber lights. The Rover shook and hummed as it reached its limit and the steering-wheel trembled in their father's hand. 'Pin on a badge,' he said, but Lisa was clinging on for her life.

185

Eventually signs for Sandown Park appeared and the country roads thickened with cars slowing for a parking space. Their father shifted the Rover into the middle of the road, roared along the broken line between the lanes of traffic and slipped through the entrance to the first car park, where within a fraction of his wing mirror he manoeuvred into a free space seconds ahead of a Bentley. The driver hooted violently and two red setters with identical and hostile eyes set up an indignant bark. Lisa, Ruby and their father leapt out and, pinning on their badges, ran away across the field in the direction of the race track.

They crossed the road and were walking through a gate marked 'Members' entrance' when two men in official uniforms closed in on them. 'Excuse me, sir,' one of them said and Lisa hoped that her father would resist using the French accent he had been practising throughout the drive. He looked shiftily out through the blue lenses of Ruby's glasses and failed to answer at all. 'Excuse me, sir, but you must be wearing a tie to go beyond this point.' Their father raised his hands to his throat and a look of amazement crossed his face.

'How extraordinary,' he said in the Queen's most precise English, 'it must have slipped off.' Lisa looked at the clock on the wall of the building opposite. There were three minutes to go. He turned to Ruby and raised his eyebrows above the glasses.

'No,' Ruby said. 'And anyway there isn't time.'

'They have ties for sale in the gift shop,' the second official offered helpfully and before he had finished his sentence their father had disappeared into a white boarded hut. He reappeared seconds later with a shiny maroon tie in a long plastic box. He tore off the wrapping, and holding up the tie as if it were a pass, pushed past the guards who were busy scanning the crowd for similar offenders. Lisa and Ruby followed him at a run.

The horses were prancing and reeling at the starting-post as they found a space high up on the tiered stands and pressed themselves against the rails. It was a startling spring day and the colours of the jockeys' caps spun in the light. 'Number eight,' their father pointed, and Lisa followed his gaze to a beautiful rust-brown horse. A white-and-blue-clad jockey perched in the saddle, leaning along the horse's neck in one last-minute conversation. The horse was Irish, was six years old and was named Balliglasson.

'The going's good and that's what she likes,' their father was saying as a loudspeaker boomed, 'And they're off!'

There were six horses in the race and they all started in a throng, picking up speed as they galloped neck and neck, their hooves flaying wildly and their backs arched. Balliglasson fell behind a little at the first jump and a whole sea of people rose to their feet and growled in low and desperate tones, 'Come on.' Their father remained silent, his eyes fixed on the horse as it began to reclaim lost ground. At the next fence it stretched its front legs and leapt into third place. Ruby gripped Lisa's arm. The loudspeaker was keeping up an urgent commentary. Then a horse fell, throwing its rider, and, picking itself up, raced on alone. It forced the winning horse to one side and Balliglasson seized her chance and roared into the lead. Lisa glanced over at her father. He was as still and white as a statue. Her blood danced in her veins. 'We're going to win, we're going to win,' she sang under her breath, immune to the ferocious grip of Ruby's fingers, numbing her arm just above the elbow. The horses turned into the far straight and raced out of view to anyone without binoculars. Every ear was strained for the commentary, which to Lisa was an unintelligible tumbling of names and numbers with the occasional audible sound of Balliglasson. When the race swept back into sight, three of the horses had fallen behind. A hush fell over the crowd. It was Balliglasson running in a two-horse race with Crimson Creek. They swept over a jump, keeping perfect pace with one another. The voices of the crowd were urgent. 'Come on, come on,' they called, drawing out the sounds between clenched teeth, and the men punched their fists into the air at any sign of hope. Lisa could see the two frantic jockeys raising up their whips as they leapt the final fence and thundered on to the home run. A bell began to ring and the commentary fell over itself with the speed of its recital. 'Go on,' Lisa heard herself murmur, as Balliglasson flew like a leopard towards the finish. Everyone was on their feet yelling and pleading and urging their horse on. Many had their own private messages and the names of the jockeys on their lips. As Lisa watched, her hands clasping the rail, the long stretched neck of Balliglasson glided across the finishing-line a split second before her rival. The race was over. The crowd shook itself silent as if woken from a trance, and some of the men mumbled into their coats and looked around with sheepish and unfocused eyes.

'It'll be a photo finish,' their father said, the colour flooding back into his face. But they knew who had won. Ruby let go of Lisa's arm and they went to hear the final decision on the race-track television.

Lisa, Ruby and their father went for tea to celebrate. They ate slivers of white bread sandwiches, fruit cake and scones with jam and clotted cream. They had to ask for a second large pot of tea and another jug of boiling water. Their father kept his beret and his glasses on throughout the meal. Full and warm and victorious, they walked back across the field to the Rover, and sailed in a haze of glory towards London.

Their father stopped at a betting-shop near Ladbroke Grove and collected his winnings. He flicked up two fifty-pound notes from the top of a fat pile and slid them out from under their elastic band. He handed them to Ruby. 'Thanks, Dad,' she said.

He gave Lisa the same. 'A hundred pounds!'

'On condition you spend it all today.' Ruby laughed and pinched her.

Their father parked his car, got out and stretched. He removed his disguise and threw it into the back with Ruby's other belongings. 'What are your plans?' he asked.

Ruby fished out her glasses and perched them on top of her head. 'I'll leave everything in the boot,' she said decisively, 'and then you'll *have* to drive me to the airport.'

Their father smiled, said goodbye and retreated up the steps and into his flat. As they walked away, they could see him at the window talking to someone on the telephone.

Ruby suggested they go into the West End and spend as much of their money as they could before closing-time. Lisa had already started to dream of how she might rearrange her treasure box to incorporate the notes, but Ruby was insistent. She hailed a cab. 'South Molton

Street,' she ordered grandly, but she remained perched on the edge of her seat.

'Where are you going?' Lisa asked, sliding forward to join her.

Ruby glanced out of the window. 'Dad's got a friend whose going to give me a job.'

'Where?'

'Argentina somewhere.' She smiled and bit sharply at the end of her nail.

'Doing what?'

'I've no idea.'

They were weaving their way into town. Lisa squeezed her sister's hand and tried to imagine what someone like Ruby would do in Argentina. She imagined her in the back yard of a ranch overseeing wild horses, counting out the lengths of time the campanero cowboys could stay on. She smiled to think of the accent Ruby would adopt. 'Will you be all right?' she asked, and when Ruby didn't answer, Lisa rephrased her question. 'Will you be staying on a hacienda?'

'I doubt it.' The taxi was on Oxford Street and Ruby was busy peering into shop windows. 'Let's get out here,' she said, and the taxi pulled up with a screech of brakes. They were across the pavement from the main revolving doors of Selfridges.

Lisa followed Ruby across the rich scented floor of leather goods – wallets and handbags and snakeskin purses – and on into the dizzying world of cosmetics, where the girls smiled coldly out at them from behind their counters. They had only ten minutes before the shop was due to close and they set off at a run for Women's Fashions.

Ruby's style had become somewhat jumbled since her incarceration in Hanworth Hospital. The precision of her earlier code of dress was gone, and even her accent had lost its edge. Occasionally a faint trace of Christine's south London lilt slipped through, and the odd, incongruous Liverpudlian expression, but mostly, today, she sounded like her old forgotten self.

Ruby pushed her way past racks of satin blouses and lambswool, pearl-buttoned cardigans. She ran her fingers through sheaves of flowery dresses and tried on an ankle-length, engine-red coat.

'What are you after?' Lisa asked her. The shop was getting ready to close. Smart, middle-aged manageresses rattled their tills and eyed them with impatience.

'Quick.' Ruby pulled Lisa by the arm, dragging her through a room of polka-dotted party dresses. 'Over here.' And through an arch she caught a glimpse of the shoe department. It was a shoe display so elegant it took her breath away. Shoes, slippers and boots were arranged on shelves of glass like triple-layered trays of cake. There were gold and silver pumps, straight-legged, two-tone riding boots and a centrepiece of stilettos in turquoise and lemon-yellow. Lisa saw a pair of red and blue suede ankle boots set jauntily on a podium. They were laced with ribbon and tied in a wide satin bow. Lisa shook herself free of Ruby's grasp and ran towards them. She knelt down in the thick carpet and, clutching a boot in each hand, began loosening the ribbons. The shop assistant stood over her. 'Do you require assistance, madam?' He was staring haughtily down at her discarded shoe.

'How much are they?' Lisa slipped her foot into place. They were a perfect fit.

The shop assistant averted his eyes. 'Forty-seven pounds and fifty pence.'

'We'll take them,' Ruby said from behind his shoulder.

He jumped imperceptibly and glanced at his watch as if he might just refuse to serve them. 'Cash or account?' he conceded.

'Cash.' Lisa fumbled in her pocket. 'I think I'll keep them on.'

Lisa's old shoes were wrapped in clean white tissue and laid aside in a cardboard box. 'Aren't you going to get anything?' she asked Ruby as the escalator returned them to the perfumed haze of the lower floor.

Ruby held out a slinky, open carrier bag. 'What do you think?' Inside was a minute orange bikini held together with circles of hollow gold.

'For Argentina?' Lisa tried to reappraise her vision of a working holiday. Ruby nodded. 'You never know.'

Ruby had a long-standing arrangement to meet up with Tom. 'I've got a lot of catching up to do.' She rustled the money in her pocket and grinned.

Lisa gripped her arm. She wanted to plead with her to stay away. 'What time is your plane, anyway?'

'Not till tomorrow night. Listen, why don't you come along?'

'What? Where?'

'To Tom's.'

She loosened her hold. 'I couldn't. I mean, it's just . . . I've . . . I'm meant to meet someone.'

Ruby began to move away. 'Well, I'll be seeing you.'

'What shall I tell Mum?'

Ruby was flailing her arms at an approaching taxi. She didn't appear to have heard.

'What shall I tell Mum?' Lisa shouted after her, but Ruby had skipped out into the middle of the road and was negotiating her fare.

*

Lisa walked down Oxford Street with her eyes fixed on the points of her boots. The red and blue diamonds of their suede toes dazzled her. They made her feet look oversized, as if with one stride they might take her in a giant leap over the moon. It was only now she was outside that she realized how little they went with the rest of her clothes. I'm meant to meet someone, she thought guiltily, examining her lie, and then it occurred to her that this might not be a lie, but a sign that the night destined for her reunion with Quentin had arrived. Over the weeks she had been taking secret bus journeys through Islington, pressing her face to the window as she passed the pub where they had met, and scanning the crowd outside the late-night cinema from the safety of the upper deck. On each occasion she had arrived home without so much as a glimpse of him, but holding steadfastly to the belief that the longer she stayed out of Quentin's way the more he was likely to miss her.

It was still early when she arrived at the pub. She stood almost alone with her back to the bar and sent out quick, shooting glances to check that it wasn't Quentin lounging in an alcove or standing jammed into a corner with a pint of Guinness. She cradled her drink, keeping the fingers of her hand welded over it like a lid. Someone waved at her from the other side of the pub. Her heart leapt and she looked abruptly away. The wave was followed by a whistle. The type of whistle you hear in a park that demands to be obeyed. Lisa began to turn slowly around and away, and as she turned, she glanced into the long, low mirror behind the bar, where she saw, striding towards her with a wide grin and a greased, black curl on his forehead, the jaunty, ice-cool figure of Jimmy Bright.

'Ruby!' he exclaimed. 'Ruby,' and before she had time to correct his mistake, he had clasped her in his arms and was jamming his tongue into her ear.

'Jimmy, get off,' she squirmed, not wanting to create a scene. 'Jimmy, it's me, it's Lisa.'

Jimmy refused to believe her. 'Ruby,' he said, 'you can't fool me. Don't think you can play those damn dirty tricks on me.' He curled his lip at her. 'Who am I?' he demanded, holding her by the shoulders.

Lisa couldn't help smiling at the irony of his question.

'Jimmy,' she answered. 'Jimmy Bright.'

Jimmy leant close in to her. 'Demon Lover,' he crooned, and he tried to take a bite out of her neck. The jukebox was playing 'Little Red Rooster' and he began to waltz her slowly on the spot. Lisa stumbled against his feet.

She tried again. 'I'm Ruby's sister, I'm Lisa, it's an easy mistake to make, people are always getting us mixed up.'

Jimmy continued to hold her close, and they danced on in silence. 'Oh Ru-ubeeey, don't take your love to town,' he sang in the break between records.

'Lisa,' she corrected him.

'Oh Ru-ubeey,' and then he opened his eyes wide. 'Only teasing,' he said, and he let her go. 'See you around, kiddo, and, if you remember, give my regards to Big Bad Sis.' He winked at her, and, as she watched, he walked away across the pub and with both hands in his pockets kicked open the heavy wooden door and sauntered out on to the street.

Lisa gulped down her drink. It was a small measure of vodka without ice or mixers. It made her feel hot and cold and as if she had a right to be there. She looked around more openly now for Quentin, even retracing her steps to the ladies' loo in the hope of invoking the lucky spirit of their first encounter, but, hard as she searched, she knew sooner or later she would have to admit that he was not there.

When Lisa arrived home, the heady smell of a baking cake filled the flat. The kitchen table was spread with a cloth and set for four.

'Who goes there?' Max called out to her from his camp between the bunk beds. 'Enter at your peril,' he snarled as she peered between the drapes and blankets of his cave. She noticed that he had drawn a small army of pencil-thin soldiers on the wall beside his pillow. They had worryingly long noses that could even be snouts, and tall, foxy ears. They were heading into battle with their shields held out in front of them.

Marguerite had cleared herself a space between the supper plates and was writing furiously. She had started an Open University course in the New Year, and at the end of each month a general panic ensued as to whether or not she would be able to complete her essay on time. She would have to study for six years to collect enough credits to get a degree and this, Lisa knew, was her intention.

Marguerite looked up expectantly. 'Where's Ruby?' Her cheeks were flushed.

'Ruby?'

'Ruby,' she insisted. There were flowers on the draining-board and Lisa noticed that her mother had dressed up. She had changed out of her uniform of faded corduroy and hand-knitted jumpers and was wearing a black-beaded dress and makeup, brown eyeshadow with golden specks, and a smudge of cherry lipstick. It didn't suit her. Marguerite stood up and strained her eyes into the dimness of the hall. 'Ruby?'

Lisa blindly followed her gaze.

'Well, where is she?' Marguerite's voice rose and her pad of paper slid off the table. The loose leaves of her notes flew across the floor. 'Where is she?'

'I don't know.' Lisa wanted to run. Something was boiling over on the stove.

'They sent a letter. They said to expect her home.' Marguerite was shouting an inch away from her face. 'Talk to me. Don't just stand there like . . . like some great lummox.' Lisa's head was spinning. Her ears had filled up with a dead weight that made it hard to decipher one word from another. She fought for an answer. The right answer. She could see her mother's eyes tearing into her. She could see that at any moment the hard lines of her face would dissolve into a mesh of tears. Lisa could come up with nothing. She gripped her stomach. She froze in the breath of silence that ensued, and then, as if she had been stabbed, she let out a low, strangled cry.

'What is it?'

Lisa curled over and began to sink towards the floor.

'What is it?' Marguerite was at her side. 'What is it, my darling?' Her voice was gentle now and under control. The animal behind her eyes had fled.

'I've got a pain,' she sobbed, 'a terrible pain.' She allowed herself to sink against her mother, her back bending in an arc of tears.

'Try and tell me where it is.'

Lisa placed her hand across her stomach and pressed. She winced in agony. Now that she put her mind to it there was a pain. A dull, comforting pain that she clung to. Warm tears slipped down her face and fell into her mouth.

Marguerite found a hankie and helped her to bed. 'I'm sorry to draw you into my troubles.' Lisa spluttered and gulped to let her know it was all right. But her mother insisted. 'It's wrong of me. It's wrong, and I'll try not to do it again. I promise.'

Lisa didn't speak. She felt calm and very tired. She lay under the covers with a hot-water bottle pressed against her side and listened while Marguerite read Max his bedtime story.

Lisa stayed in bed the whole of the next day. Max, under orders to keep quiet, tiptoed around her, regaling her with whispered lists of fly hooks, and the weight and size of fish he intended to catch. He told her about Nermil, his favourite enemy, and asked her countless questions about God. Max was learning about God at school. How God was the all-seeing Father. 'Nowadays,' Max said, 'God really gets on my nerves.'

'Why's that?'

Max sighed. 'He keeps watching when I'm on the toilet,' and he kicked his feet grumpily against the edge of her bed.

Marguerite tempted her with tinned soup and grapes. She plied her with slices of cake. 'I had no idea how thin you'd got,' she frowned. 'Just scrape off the burnt bits and it's still delicious. How's the pain?'

Lisa pressed and prodded at her stomach. 'It comes and goes.'

Marguerite swore that first thing Monday morning she would make an appointment for Lisa with the doctor.

Lisa wondered how her mother would find out about Ruby going to Argentina if she wasn't the one to tell her. She worried that her father would forget it was him who was supposed to be driving her to the airport. Ruby would have to leave without her luggage. She would arrive with nothing but her orange bikini and a fifty-pound note. When she started on these thoughts, a pain really did twist inside her stomach and she called out for a drink and a fresh hot-water bottle.

'My poor darling.' Marguerite plumped up her pillows. 'Just lie still, and don't worry about a thing.'

Lisa closed her eyes.

'Lummox,' Max whispered in her ear, and she smiled. Whatever happened now she had an alibi.

When Lisa woke up, it was dark and the door to her room was shut. She could hear voices, gritty and dissenting, lowered in the kitchen. There was a man's voice she didn't recognize. It wasn't the caretaker, or Steen. Lisa crept across the room, opened her door and looked out. She started back. Ruby was there, talking and twisting her fingers, and just behind her, leaning up against the fridge, was her father. He looked small and suspicious and strangely out of place.

Lisa leapt back into bed. 'Mum,' she called out, and she sat up bleary-eyed, as if she had that second woken.

Marguerite tiptoed into the room. 'How are you feeling?'

Lisa hugged her stomach and put on a brave face.

Marguerite sat on the edge of the bed. 'Ruby's going away for a little while.' She switched on a lamp. 'She's come to say goodbye.'

Ruby put her head round the door and smiled. 'Hasta la vista.' She came over and hugged Lisa. 'Dad's going to take you to a specialist.' She lowered her voice. 'They're terribly worried.'

Lisa felt her eyes brim over. She fumbled under her pillow for a handkerchief. 'Will you write?'

'I suppose it's because you're never, ever ill,' Ruby added wistfully.

Their father appeared in the doorway. 'We'd better make a move.' He smiled at Lisa. 'I'll be in touch.'

'I'll be in touch tomorrow,' she heard him tell Marguerite as she opened the front door to them.

'Bye, Mum,' Ruby said, and there was a pause in which Lisa thought she heard her mother sniff. 'Goodbye, Max. And Max,' she called up the stairs, 'adios, bandito.'

Max pelted her with a machine-gun round of friendly fire.

On the afternoon of the next day a telegram arrived. It was from Lisa's father and contained what they could only assume were details of a doctor's appointment. MEET GROSVENOR HOTEL 11 A.M. TUESDAY.

Lisa stayed in bed and attempted to catch up on her college work. She was doing a project on ancient Greek theatre and was behind by several weeks. Marguerite brought her own work through from the kitchen to keep her company, she had started with myth, and moved on to music. Lisa flicked through her mother's Open University pamphlets. They were so much clearer than the dusty pile of library books heaped up by her bed. 'What are you doing next?'

Marguerite wasn't sure. She went through to the bedroom and scooped a brown-paper package from under the bed. 'Drama!' She pulled the pamphlets free and let them fall on to Lisa's lap. 'See if there's anything helpful in there.'

There was an entire section on Greek theatre. She sat up in bed and copied happily. She discovered exactly how a fifth-century-BC production of *Oedipus Rex* would have been staged, and that the three actors used to play the parts were the protagonist, the deuteragonist and the tritagonist. She traced illustrations of the reconstructed amphitheatre at Epidaurus, of the *thymele*, the *skene* and the *parados*, and of the masks worn by the players.

Marguerite beamed. 'And who says I'm not a good mother?'

Lisa found a section on the open-air, all-night orgies indulged in by the followers of the god Dionysus and continued to copy.

The Grosvenor Hotel was at the back of Victoria station and, like the cartoon cinema, had been a landmark for Lisa as a child. For many years she had been under the impression, when she looked up at the giant letters of its name, that it was not the Grosvenor but the Gronsovenor Hotel. A tendency towards dyslexia, especially at a distance, often distorted the words that Lisa saw elongated across London, and added to the lasting impression they made on her. 'What's Harry's bristle cream?' she had once asked her father, pointing at a wall-sized advertisement through the open window of a taxi, and he had laughed until the tears ran down his face. 'Harry's bristle cream?' he repeated, his voice hoarse, and he tousled her hair in admiration. She joined in his laughter and her eyes danced. Ruby laughed too and was never again so quick to correct her. 'It's not the Gronsovenor, nitwit,' she had been in the habit of saying, 'it's the Gross Venor!' It was only now Lisa realized with some amusement that it was pronounced with a silent S and they had both been wrong.

Lisa's father was standing on the steps reading the sports pages of a paper. She was surprised to see him there a few minutes before eleven.

'Shall we go?' he asked when he saw her, and he hailed a taxi. 'How are you feeling?'

'It comes and goes,' she told him with a wince. She had managed to convince herself of this. The more she

202

dwelt on it the more strongly she believed in the vivid, stabbing pains that she described.

The doctor was not a specialist, but the doctor of a friend of Lisa's father. The surgery was on the ground floor of a newly painted house five minutes from Victoria. There were magazines piled high on tables between three sofas, and a secretary who sat typing at a desk in the centre of the room.

'Lisa, how nice to meet you,' the doctor smiled, and held the door for her. He ushered her towards a chair. 'And what can I do for you?' He was a small man with a shiny, hairless head.

Lisa didn't know where to start.

'You have been suffering from stomach pains?' he encouraged.

Lisa blinked. She was frightened that if she opened her mouth she might start to cry.

'Apparently they came on quite suddenly, is this right?' He pushed a box of tissues towards her. 'It's all right, everyone feels a bit sorry for themselves when they come to see me.'

Lisa tried to smile and immediately burst into tears. He pushed the box closer and waited for her to stop.

'If you'd like to slip off your things, jump up on the bed, and I'll have a look at you.'

Lisa obediently blew her nose. She lay on the cold, hygenic roll of paper towel and kept her eyes open while the doctor prodded and pressed at her stomach. She watched his face for signs of suspicion. For signs that he might tell on her. Tell her off for wasting his valuable time. Not to mention her father's. 'Ow,' she gasped as her stomach tightened and the doctor pushed his thumb deep in beside her hip bone.

'If you'd like to get dressed.'

Lisa stumbled into her clothes.

'How old are you, my dear?'

'Sixteen.'

'Could you tell me the date of your last period?'

Lisa couldn't remember. 'Ages ago.' She looked at him, startled. 'You don't think I'm pregnant, do you?'

The doctor glanced up, the warmth gone from his eyes. 'Do you have reason to think you might be?'

'No.' Lisa was adamant.

'Well then.' The doctor went to the door and called her father in. 'I don't think there is anything seriously wrong,' he told him, 'but I do think it would be advisable to consult a specialist.'

Lisa felt her cheeks burning with relief.

'I could ask my secretary to make an appointment.'

Lisa and her father both nodded their agreement, and while they waited he paid her bill with cash.

They went for lunch at the fish restaurant in Chinatown where Lisa's father was a regular.

'We could try somewhere else if you'd prefer?'

Lisa assumed he was referring to the Wimpy, Notting Hill, and insisted she was happy where they were.

'You'll be pleased to know,' he told her, 'that oysters are out of season.'

Lisa laughed and studied the menu. She chose corned beef hash with a poached egg. Her father smiled indulgently and ordered salmon.

'How are you getting on with your acting?' he asked.

'All right.'

'It's only that I was thinking, when I was young, and fanatical about horses, the one person I wanted to meet was a famous jockey, Gordon Richards or Lester Piggott.'

'And did you?'

'I did eventually. I hung around so much they gave me a job as a stable-lad.' He paused. 'I had wanted to be a jockey myself.'

Lisa stopped eating. 'Why didn't you?'

'Too tall. I grew too tall. It can happen to anyone. Anyway, I was thinking, presuming you don't know any, that you might like to meet an actor?'

Lisa thought of the boy from *Scum* and the actors she had seen at the party. 'No,' she said. 'I don't know any.'

'There's an actor who drinks at a club I go to. I don't know his name but I get the feeling he's rather well thought of. Quite famous. If you'd like, I could arrange for you to meet him.'

'Could you?' Lisa's imagination exploded at the thought of a possible tea with Dr Who or the Saint. It might even be possible to ask the actor to meet her from college. She tried to picture the faces of the Full Time Speech and Drama course when they saw Marlon Brando waiting for her in the foyer. 'Would you be there too?' she asked, the enormity of the situation sinking in on her, and her father assured her that he would.

It was only when they'd eaten, and there was a silence as they pondered on whether to have pudding or not, that Lisa realized they had sat through an entire lunch without a mention of Ruby. 'I expect Ruby will have arrived in Argentina by now,' she cut in quickly to redress the balance.

Her father ordered fresh raspberries. 'She most

certainly should have, unless she hijacked the plane and made a forced landing in New York.'

They both laughed and Lisa asked the waiter for chocolate cake with a double portion of ice cream.

Marguerite had decided she would accompany Lisa when her appointment with the specialist came round. Lisa sweated in dread at the thought of both her parents sitting, side by side, in the interminable shuffling hush of a hospital waiting-room. She tried to talk her out of it, but Marguerite was adamant.

On the morning of the appointed day a threatening, high-pitched ringing started up in her ears. 'NO.' She shook her head. 'No, it's not a good idea,' and she clutched her stomach and groaned to back up her outburst.

Marguerite rushed to put the kettle on. She stirred honey into camomile tea and, once Lisa was wrapped in blankets and propped up with a pillow, she calmly agreed to stay behind.

The whine in Lisa's ears died. She felt as light as air. She grinned at her mother. 'You mustn't worry about me,' she said, and she added silently to herself with a little skip of her heart, 'I'm all right. I'm all right. I'm going to be all right.'

The hospital was a private hospital and there was not the pale green waiting-room she had anticipated. She was shown into a small room like an office and given a long, cold drink the consistency of milk shake. The doctor watched it travel through her intestine on a television screen.

He looked over at Lisa and raised his eyebrows. He was young and clean-shaven with perfectly manicured nails. 'Do you smoke?' Lisa squirmed, but he didn't wait for an answer. 'Give up. You hear me? You have an extremely sensitive system and any irritant could have devastating effects.'

Lisa pulled down her jumper and came and sat in the spare chair at his desk. She felt giddy with his words and sick with the lead lying at the bottom of her stomach.

'From now on, you will eat three meals a day.' He looked at her sternly, and he began to write out a prescription. She was to mix a sachet of powder with a full glass of water and drink it before each meal. After each meal she was to take a pill. 'Morning, midday and evening.'

Lisa opened her mouth to protest, but the doctor shook the creases out of his trousers and showed her to the door.

'Three meals a day,' she told her father when she eventually found him sprawled across a leather sofa reading a copy of *Country Life*. 'I've heard worse,' he said, and he took her hand and led her out across the sea of carpet.

Lisa sat in the canteen with Eugene and Janey. They watched as she tore the top off a sachet of medicine and poured its contents into a plastic beaker. It frothed and fizzed and finally dissolved into a glutinous orange drink, which Lisa proceeded to gulp down. 'I haven't been well,' she told them as she drained her glass. She had to wait five minutes before she could start on her paper plate of ravioli.

'Pete's very impressed with your project,' Janey said. 'I overheard him talking to Denise.'

'Really?' Lisa smiled guiltily.

'He said if your practical comes up to the same standard, you could get an A in your Drama which would mean you were eligible for a full grant to go to drama school. What pieces are you doing?'

'I don't know.'

Janey had chosen hers already. Beatie from *Roots* by Arnold Wesker. And for her classical, Juliet's balcony speech.

'I suppose I could do something from the *Three Sisters*.'

'I'm a seagull, I'm a seagull, no, no, I'm an actress.' Eugene mimicked the exact speech she had in mind with his hand fluttering in mock melodrama across his brow.

Janey's face lit up. 'Listen, we've got time before the next lesson, why don't we walk down to RADA and collect some application forms? You have to apply now if you want to be seen next year. When's your birthday?'

'August.'

'Right, so you'll be seventeen by the time they see you. You can pretend you're eighteen, and by the time you get a place you nearly will be.'

'If I get in.'

'You've got a better chance than I have. At least to them you're not a Paki with a Purley accent. And you've got the chance of a grant.'

Lisa remembered and took her after-meal pill.

'Coming, Eugene?'

'You think I want to waste my time with drama school?' According to Eugene, he had made important contacts during his two and a half years as an usher. 'I shall audition for the top West End shows.' He bared his teeth in a broad, white smile and tapped a double shuffle under the table. His singing followed them as they hurried from the canteen.

RADA was a twenty-minute walk from their college. Janey knew of someone who had been accepted there several years ago, but who had been unable to get a grant.

'From our course?'

'Yes.'

'Accepted at RADA!' Lisa was incredulous.

'And then not to be able to go,' Janey added sorrowfully. 'It depends on what borough you live in. Some boroughs are more stingy than others. I've heard Purley is one of the worst.'

Lisa had often walked into the West End with groups of girls from the Full Time Speech and Drama course. The lunch hour at college had stretched with each term so that often the morning and the afternoon classes were divided by over two hours. The route they took in order to windowshop or browse in the shops on Tottenham Court Road invariably led past the stone façade of RADA. 'Royal Acadamy of Dramatic Art,' they all murmured reverentially as they passed. Until now it had never occurred to Lisa that she might be eligible to apply.

Lisa and Janey pushed open the door and wandered into the hall. There was a wall of gold-tinted glass inscribed with the names of graduating students. Lisa didn't recognize any of them, not having been brought up with television, but Janey pointed and gasped as her eyes travelled down the list.

Lisa looked around hopefully for a real-life student. She expected to see girls in leotards with curling, pre-Raphaelite hair, and men who looked like James Dean, but there was no one about. In fact RADA had finished early for Easter. They found the office and collected an application form each. The application forms came with a suggestion sheet for students preparing speeches. One classical, preferably Shakespeare. One modern. Not exceeding three minutes. At the bottom of the page was an asterisked note. 'Actresses: We would be grateful if applicants could refrain from preparing Beatie from *Roots*, and to see another balcony scene from *Romeo and Juliet* would not be helpful.'

Janey was mortified, and they walked back to college in silence.

That evening as Lisa neared home, passing fearlessly through the short cut to emerge unscathed at the top of the ramp, she saw her mother's anxious face watching out for her from the front window of their flat.

Marguerite waved frantically and disappeared from view. Lisa raced across Peerless Street and bumped into her on the pavement.

'Lisa, we've been offered a flat.' She had come out without her shoes.

Lisa shook her head in disbelief.

'We've been offered a council flat. With three bedrooms. Kitchen and sitting-room!'

'And bathroom?'

'And bathroom, of course.' And they hugged each other and ran back up the stairs to their landing. In a spirit of celebration they kicked open the front door without bothering to search their pockets for a key.

The next morning early, Marguerite, Lisa and Max put on their best clothes and went to inspect their new home. It was on the other side of the Old Street roundabout, a little further east towards the City. The flat was a miniature house within a modern block of maisonettes. The doors were painted alternately in olive-green and brown, and the windows were cut in single panes of glass.

'Is this it?' Lisa asked once they were inside.

Marguerite looked sternly at her. 'It's permanent.'

The sitting-room was L-shaped and had a long, sliding window that looked over a graveyard. Outside was a narrow, concrete slip of balcony wide enough to hang a single line of washing.

A permanent home! Lisa thought, and looked over at her mother. Marguerite was rapping at the wall around the gas fire in the hope of locating a hidden flue.

Lisa sighed, and pushed past her. Upstairs there were three square bedrooms with low ceilings and a small, tilting window in each.

Max ran into the bathroom and lay down in the bath. Lisa had told him how, when she was his age, she had spent time pretending to be dead. Max had taken this particular game to heart and practised it whenever he remembered. Lisa, as a child, had lain for what seemed like hours behind a sofa or under a bed, patiently waiting for someone to discover her, but Max, the minute he had closed his eyes, demanded ferociously that all present rush to his aid.

Lisa stood over him now and put her finger to her lips. 'Max, shhh,' she said urgently. He had one eye open and she knew that he could see her.

'Were you worried?' he asked, leaping to his feet.

Lisa lifted him out of the bath. 'The idea,' she told him for the hundredth time, 'is to stay silent for as long as you possibly can. No one should even hear you squeak.'

Max slid rebelliously to the floor. He shot her a scornful, disappointed glance. Lisa supposed that he probably had stayed silent for as long as he possibly could.

Lisa walked back downstairs. The staircase was short and squat with a centre strip just waiting to be carpeted. Inside the kitchen there were matching rows of cupboards, below and above the sink, and new, flecked lino that fitted tightly into every corner. A ventilator hissed shrilly as it spun for air. Lisa found herself thinking nostalgically of Peerless Street, with its draughts and cracks and the temperamental cold tap that dripped for no reason in the middle of the night.

'We are incredibly lucky,' Marguerite told her on the walk home, 'it's practically unheard of to be rehoused so soon.' But they didn't meet each other's eye.

*

That night Lisa lay in bed and wondered if there was any way in which she would be able to stay on in Peerless Flats. With or without her mother. She ran her hand lovingly over the woodchip paper, and followed the pattern of reflected light where it fell from the window in its nightly grid, distorted on the wall. She listened for the beat of upstairs' music and the familiar creaking of their front door as the wind from the stairwell caught at its loose hinges. She imagined she knew by heart each pair of hurrying feet as they passed each other on the stairs.

Lisa woke with the word 'permanent' stinging in her thoughts. She found her mother already up, puzzling over a letter. 'This is the most extraordinary thing,' and she continued to read. Marguerite shook her head and turned the letter over. 'The most extraordinary thing.'

Lisa tried to take it out of her hands. She could see the New Swift emblem on the letterhead. 'What is it?'

'It seems' – Marguerite let her eyes travel over the sense of the letter – 'that New Swift are finally prepared to offer us somewhere to live.'

There were also two letters for Lisa. One was from Mr Bunzl, asking why she had missed her last appointment. The other was from her father. 'A hot tip for the three-thirty-five Saturday. Ascot. Will you be my guest?' Lisa smiled and folded his letter so it would fit into her treasure box.

She put off going into college and, with Max only too happy to miss another day of school, they slipped sheepishly out on to the street and headed for the bus stop. They saw Heidi folding washing in the bay window of her flat, but they didn't stop to talk. Lisa felt greedy and full of choices. She thought of Frances's soft, despairing voice as she packed up to go home to Ireland, and the

214

family on the top floor who were penalized for pouring the grease from frying-pans out of their kitchen window. It stuck like glue to the side of the building and left a cold, stale smell. They had been waiting over four years to be rehoused.

The New Swift house was on the other side of Archway and they had instructions to collect the key from Russell, a Co-op member who lived near the tube. Russell was one of the earnest, bearded men who presided so laboriously over meetings, and he directed them across the Holloway Road and on through a maze of short, Edwardian terraces inter-cut with the walls and corners of new, red-brick estates.

'Is it a modern house?' Lisa asked, but Marguerite didn't know.

'The only thing I do know is that it's temporary.' She laughed and shook her head. 'We shouldn't even be considering it.'

The Co-op house was in a cul-de-sac that crossed the railway line at the top of Hornsey Rise. It was a three-storey house with a crack across the ground-floor window and a front garden piled high with rubbish. The next-door house was derelict and boarded up.

Marguerite referred to the letter. 'Yes, this is it,' she sighed. 'And we can live here for anything up to a year and a half.'

Lisa took the key out of her hand and with some difficulty turned it in the lock. Light from a broken window in the back door flooded through the house and caught in the swirling dust dislodged by their arrival. Max ran down the passage beside the stairs, jumped over a hole in the floorboards and pulled at the handle of the back door. He pulled so hard it came away and he fell over backwards, hitting his head against the wall.

'OW,' he moaned, and Marguerite muttered a regret that she hadn't let him wear his helmet.

The back door was in fact unlocked, and swung open with a twist of the metal pin. Max picked himself up and hurtled out into the sunshine. He was heading for the row of lilac trees that grew in the broken fence between the two back gardens. Lisa caught him just in time and held him by the shoulders. Marguerite came out and joined her, and even Max stopped his struggling and stared. The garden wasn't a garden, but a rubbish dump. It was trampled and rotted and formed into a waist-high plateau of mattresses and faded plastic. Three broken-up cisterns lay half buried. Over the top, glinting in the light, lay a liberal scattering of hypodermic needles.

'Look at those exquisite lilacs,' Marguerite pointed. 'There's a white one, and that purple one there is about to burst into flower.'

'I want to climb a tree,' Max yelled, but they went back inside to explore the house.

The house was light, and dusty, and bore evidence of various ramshackle attempts at redecoration. Several bannisters were bright pink and others had been stripped and polished to their natural state. The wooden floorboards around the edges of the kitchen were painted in black and white squares, as if the lino that had once been there hadn't been quite wide enough.

They trooped into the room at the front of the house. It had a fireplace with an iron grate and was made private by the towering hedge that grew in the front garden. It cast the dark green shadow of a thousand swimming minnows across the walls. From the inside the crack in the glass didn't look so dangerous and the rubbish was out of view below the window-sill. Lisa looked sidelong at her mother.

Upstairs were two large bedrooms with sash windows that stretched from floor to ceiling and a bathroom on the landing below. At each landing the bannisters changed their colour, and as they continued up, Lisa noticed they were speckled with little blobs of shiny paint. Max was the first to arrive at the top of the stairs. 'Reinforcements!' he thundered, as he charged the door to the back bedroom.

'What is it?' Lisa called after him. He had stopped with the door half open and refused to go in.

'Reinforcements for foxes,' he muttered as if his life depended on it, and he started back down the stairs.

Marguerite pushed past them and peered into the room. She caught her breath and then as the seconds passed in silence she let it out with a long hiss between her teeth. 'Look at this.' Lisa stood on tiptoe to see over her shoulder. The smell in the room was thick and bitter and hit her like a gag. She was forced to breathe in through her mouth.

Inside the room was a mattress that looked as if it might have been retrieved from the garden. It was brown and stained and curled up at the corners. In its centre was a dank mound of blanket. Lisa knew what had stopped Max in his tracks. She could feel her own dread of what lay hidden there rising up inside her. She felt Max's fingers tapping the back of her legs.

'Look at those smelly old blankets,' she told him, swallowing her fear, and she thought she understood why it was that women had children. 'Look at those smelly old blankets with nothing inside but air.'

'Yes, it looks like whoever's been living here has certainly moved out,' Marguerite agreed and she strode

217

across the room and threw open the window. A blast of fresh spring air blew through the room and a train rumbled past on the railway line.

'It's a terribly important decision.' Marguerite locked up the house. 'A terribly important decision.'

Lisa bent her head to hide her smile. It was just a matter of time before her mother gave in to the challenge. 'We could hire a skip,' she suggested, 'and wheel the rubbish along the downstairs corridor and out through the front door. If we asked everyone we know to help, it would only take a couple of days.'

'We could keep bees, at the back of the garden.' Marguerite's eyes began to shine. 'I rather fancy being a member of the Inner London Bee-keeping Society.'

Max danced ahead of them. 'Do foxes climb trees?'

'Or we could get a cat.'

'It is possible' – Marguerite was entering into the spirit of adventure – 'the Co-Op may let us have it for longer than they say.'

'Anything can happen in a year and a half,' Lisa encouraged. She was thinking about the white branches of the lilac brushing up against the bathroom window. In winter she could make a wood fire in her bedroom, and hang thick velvet curtains to block out the draught. Quentin, who lived just over the hill, might tap his fingers on the glass to wake her in the middle of one night.

Marguerite took her arm. 'But I thought it was what you always wanted. A permanent home.'

'It was.'

Max danced ahead of them in a wild zigzag across the pavement. 'I'll plant an army in the garden,' he yelled joyously.